BEST LOVED BOOKS
FOR YOUNG READERS

Kidnapped

The Adventures of David Balfour

A CONDENSATION OF THE BOOK BY

Robert Louis Stevenson

Illustrated by N. C. Wyeth

CHOICE PUBLISHING, INC.

New York

PRODUCED IN ASSOCIATION WITH MEDIA PROJECTS INCORPORATED

Executive Editor, Carter Smith
Managing Editor, Jeanette Mall
Project Editor, Jacqueline Ogburn
Associate Editor, Charles Wills
Contributing Editor, Beth Passaro
Art Director, Bernard Schleifer

Library of Congress Catalog Number: 88-63358
ISBN: 0-945260-32-6

This 1989 edition is published and distributed by Choice Publishing, Inc.,
Great Neck, NY 11021, with permission of The Reader's Digest Association, Inc.

Manufactured in the United States of America.

10 9 8 7 6 5 4 3 2

Foreword

THIS IS THE thrilling tale of an orphan boy's stolen inheritance, his kidnaping, and his long, perilous flight through the Scottish Highlands to claim his own. It is set in the tumultuous times of the mid-eighteenth century, when in mountain hideaways proud clansmen carried on bitter feuds, and desperate Jacobites, still smarting from their defeat by the English at Culloden, plotted under the exiled Bonnie Prince Charlie to return his Stuart line to the throne of Great Britain.

The story of young David Balfour, beset by mortal dangers and torn between his loyalty to King George and to a daring Jacobite friend, could only have been told by a writer who was both a student of the period and a romantic at heart. Robert Louis Balfour Stevenson (1850–1894) loved his native Scotland, knew its history, and understood the Scottish mind and heart. That he was also a romantic, his own life amply demonstrated—if only that he fell in love with an American woman, Fannie Osbourne, and followed her halfway around the world to California, by steerage and immigrant train, to bring her back to Scotland as his bride. In later years he took her with him to live in Samoa, in the South Pacific; and it was there he died.

The further adventures of the hero of *Kidnapped* are related in its sequel, *David Balfour*. Among the other books for which Stevenson will always be remembered are *Treasure Island*, *The Strange Case of Dr. Jekyll and Mr. Hyde*, and *A Child's Garden of Verses*.

CHAPTER I

I set off upon my journey to the house of Shaws

I WILL BEGIN THE STORY of my adventures with a certain morning early in the month of June, the year of grace 1751, when I took the key for the last time out of the door of my father's house. The sun began to shine upon the summit of the hills as I went down the road; and by the time I had come as far as the manse, the blackbirds were whistling in the garden lilacs, and the mist that hung around the valley in the time of the dawn was beginning to arise and die away.

Mr. Campbell, the minister of Essendean, was waiting for me by his garden gate. He asked me if I had breakfasted, and hearing that I lacked for nothing, took my hand in both of his and clapped it kindly under his arm.

"Well, Davie, lad," said he, "I will go with you as far as the ford, to set you on the way." We began to walk forward in silence.

"Are ye sorry to leave Essendean?" said he, after a while.

"Why, sir," said I, "if I knew where I was going or what was likely to become of me, I would tell you candidly. Essendean is a good place, and I have been very happy here. But I have never been anywhere else, and, to speak truth, if I thought I had a chance to better myself where I was going, I would go with a good will."

"Very well, Davie," said Mr. Campbell. "Then it behoves me to tell your fortune; or so far as I may. After your mother died, and

I

your father began to sicken for his end, he gave me a certain letter, which he said was your inheritance. 'So soon,' said he, 'as I am gone, and the house disposed of, give my boy this letter, and start him off to the house of Shaws, not far from Cramond. That is the place I came from, and it befits that my boy should return there.'"

"The house of Shaws!" I cried. "What had my poor father to do with the house of Shaws?"

"Nay," said Mr. Campbell, "who can tell that? But the name of that family, Davie boy, is the name you bear—Balfour of Shaws: an ancient, reputable house. Your father, too, was a man of learning and no man more plausibly conducted school; nor had he the manner of an ordinary schoolmaster. Indeed, as ye will remember, I took pleasure to have him to my own house to meet the gentry, all of whom had pleasure in his society. But here is the letter itself."

He gave me the letter, which was addressed: "To Ebenezer Balfour, Esq., of Shaws; this will be delivered by my son, David Balfour." My heart was beating hard at this great prospect suddenly opening before a lad of seventeen, the son of a poor country schoolmaster. "Mr. Campbell," I stammered, "if you were in my shoes, would you go?"

"Of a surety," said he, "and without pause. A lad like you should walk to Cramond, which is near Edinburgh, in two days. If the worst came to the worst, and your high relations (as I suppose them to be) should put you to the door, ye can but walk the two days back again. But I would rather hope that ye shall be well received, and, in time, come to be a great man. And here, Davie, laddie, it lies upon my conscience to set you on the right guard against the dangers of the world."

And with a very long, serious upper lip, he sat down upon a big boulder under a birch by the trackside, and put his pocket-handkerchief over his cocked hat to shelter him from the sun. There, with uplifted forefinger, he put me on my guard against a number of heresies to which I had no temptation, and urged upon me to be instant in my prayers and reading of the Bible. That done, he drew a picture of the great house to which I was bound, and how I should conduct myself there.

"Bear in mind, Davie, that, though gentle born, ye have had a country rearing. Dinnae shame us, Davie! In yon great house with all the domestics, show yourself as circumspect, as quick at the conception, and as slow of speech as any. As for the laird—remember he's the laird. I say no more: honor to whom honor. It should be a pleasure to the young to obey a laird."

"Well, sir," said I, "I promise I'll try to make it so."

"Well said," replied Mr. Campbell heartily. "And now I have a little packet which contains four things." He tugged it from his coat pocket. "The first is the little money for your father's books and furniture, which I have bought in the design of reselling at a profit to the incoming schoolmaster. The other three are gifts that Mrs. Campbell and myself would be blithe of your acceptance. The first, which is round, will likely please ye best at first; but Davie, laddie, it's but a drop of water in the sea. The second, which is flat and square and written upon, will stand by you through life, like a good staff for the road, and a good pillow to your head in sickness. As for the last, which is cubical, that'll see you, it's my prayerful wish, into a better land."

With that he got up, took off his hat, and prayed a little while aloud, and in affecting terms, for a young man setting out into the world. Then suddenly he embraced me very hard, and crying good-by to me, set off at a jog by the way that we had come. I watched him as long as he was in sight. He never stopped hurrying, nor once looked back. Then it came upon my mind that this was all his sorrow at my departure, and my conscience smote me hard because I, for my part, was overjoyed to get out of that quiet countryside.

And I sat down on the boulder the good man had just left, and opened the parcel to see the nature of my gifts. That which he had called cubical was sure enough a Bible. That which he had called round was a shilling piece; and that which was to help me both in health and sickness all my life was a little piece of coarse yellow paper. Written upon it in red ink were instructions to make Lily of the Valley Water. Beneath these, in the minister's own hand, was added: "A liquor which is good, ill or well, and whether man or woman, for it comforts the heart and strengthens the memory. For sprains, rub it in. For the colic, a great spoonful in the hour."

To be sure I laughed over this, but it was rather tremulous laughter; and I was glad to get my bundle on my staff's end and set out over the ford and up the hill.

Just as I came on the green drove road running through the heather, I took my last look of Essendean and the big rowan trees in the kirkyard where my father and my mother lay.

CHAPTER II

I make acquaintance of my uncle

ON THE FORENOON OF THE SECOND DAY, I saw the country fall away before me down to the sea and, in the midst of this descent, the city of Edinburgh smoking like a kiln. I could distinguish clearly a flag upon the castle, and ships moving in the firth; both of which brought my country heart into my mouth.

Presently I came by a shepherd and got a direction for Cramond; and so worked my way westward till I came out upon the Glasgow road. There I beheld a regiment marching to the fifes, every foot in time, with a red-faced general on a gray horse at one end, and at the other the company of Grenadiers, with their Pope's hats. The pride of life seemed to mount into my brain at the sight of the red coats and the hearing of that merry music.

A little farther on, I was in Cramond, and substituted in my inquiries the name of the house of Shaws. It was a word that seemed to surprise those of whom I sought my way. At first I thought my country habit consorted ill with the greatness of the place to which I was bound. But after two or three had given me the same look and answer, I began to take it in my head there was something strange about the Shaws itself.

To set this fear at rest, I changed the form of my inquiries and asked a fellow, coming along a lane on the shaft of his cart, if he had ever heard tell of a house called Shaws. He stopped his cart and looked at me, like the others.

"Ay," said he. "It's a big, muckle house."

"But the folk that are in it?" I asked.

"Folk?" cried he. "Are ye daft? There's nae folk there—to call folk."

"What?" says I. "Not Mr. Ebenezer?"

"There's the laird, to be sure, if it's him you're wanting," says the man. "What'll be your business, mannie?"

"I was led to think that I would get a situation," I said, looking as modest as I could.

"What?" cries the carter, in so sharp a note that his horse started. "It's nane of my affairs, but ye seem a decent lad. If ye'll take a word from me, ye'll keep clear of the Shaws."

I cannot well describe the blow this dealt to my illusions. If an hour's walking would have brought me back to Essendean, I had left my adventure then and there, and returned to Mr. Campbell's. But when I had come so far, I was bound, out of mere self-respect, to carry it through.

It was drawing on to sundown when I met a stout, dark, sour-looking woman trudging down a hill. She, when I had asked my way, accompanied me back to the summit she had just left, and pointed to a great building standing very bare upon a green in the bottom of the next valley. The low hills round about were pleasantly watered and wooded, and the crops wonderfully good; but the house itself appeared to be a ruin. No road led up to it; no smoke arose from the chimneys; nor was there any garden. My heart sank. "That!" I cried.

The woman's face lit up with anger. "That is the house of Shaws!" she cried. "Blood built it; blood stopped the building of it; blood shall bring it down. See here! I spit upon the ground, and crack my thumb at it! Black be its fall! If ye see the laird, tell him this makes the twelve hunner and nineteen time that Jennet Clouston has called down the curse on him and his house."

And the woman, whose voice had risen to a kind of hideous sing-song, turned and was gone. In those days folk still believed in

5

curses, and this one, falling like a wayside omen, took the pith out of my legs. I sat down and stared at the house of Shaws. The more I looked, the pleasanter that countryside appeared; being all set with hawthorn bushes full of flowers; the fields dotted with sheep; and yet the barrack in the midst of it went sore against my fancy.

Folk went by from the fields as I sat there but I lacked the spirit to give them a good-e'en. At last the sun went down, and then, against the yellow sky, I saw a scroll of smoke go mounting. Not much thicker than that of a candle, it still meant warmth and cookery; so I set forward by a faint grass track that brought me to stone uprights, with an unroofed lodge beside them, and coats of arms upon the top. A main entrance it was plainly meant to be, but never finished. Instead of gates of wrought iron, a pair of hurdles were tied across with a straw rope. As there were no park walls, nor any sign of avenue, the track that I was following passed on the right hand of the pillars, and went wandering on toward the house.

The nearer I got, the more it seemed like the one wing of a house that had never been finished. What should have been the inner end stood open on the upper floors. Many of the windows were unglazed, and bats flew in and out like doves out of a dovecote. In three of the lower windows, which were narrow and well barred, the light of a little fire was glimmering.

Coming forward cautiously, I heard someone rattling dishes, and a dry fitful cough. The great door, as well as I could see in the dim light, was studded with nails. I lifted my hand with a faint heart, and knocked. Then I waited. The house had fallen into silence. A whole minute passed and nothing stirred but the bats. I knocked again. By this time my ears had grown so accustomed to the quiet, that I could hear the ticking of the clock inside; but whoever was in that house kept deadly still.

I was in two minds whether to run away, but anger got the upper hand, and I began to rain kicks and buffets on the door, and to shout out for Mr. Balfour. I was in full career, when I heard the cough right overhead, and jumping back, beheld a man's head

6

in a tall nightcap, and the mouth of a blunderbuss, at one of the first-story windows.

"It's loaded," said a voice.

"I have come here with a letter," I said, "to Mr. Ebenezer Balfour of Shaws. Is he here?"

"Well," said the man with the blunderbuss, "ye can put it down upon the doorstep, and be off with ye."

"I will do no such thing," I cried. "I will deliver it into Mr. Balfour's hands. It is a letter of introduction."

"A what?" cried the voice sharply. I repeated what I had said. "Who are ye, yourself?" was the next question.

"They call me David Balfour," said I.

At that, I am sure the man started, for I heard the blunderbuss rattle on the windowsill, and after a long pause and with a curious change of voice, the next question followed: "Is your father dead?" I was so surprised at this that I could find no voice to answer, but stood staring. "Ay," the man resumed, "he'll be dead, and that'll be what brings ye chapping to my door." Another pause, and then defiantly, "Well, man, I'll let ye in."

He disappeared from the window. Presently there came a great rattling of chains and bolts, and the door was cautiously opened.

"Go into the kitchen and touch naething," said the voice, and while the person of the house set himself to replacing the defenses of the door, I groped my way forward. The kitchen fire burned up fairly bright and showed me the barest room I ever put my eyes on. Half a dozen dishes stood upon the shelves; the table was laid with a bowl of porridge, a horn spoon, and a cup of beer. There was not another thing in that great, stone-vaulted chamber but lockfast chests along the walls and a corner cupboard with a padlock.

The man rejoined me. He was a stooping, narrow-shouldered, clay-faced creature. His age might have been anything between fifty and seventy. His nightcap and the nightgown he wore over his ragged shirt were of flannel. He was long unshaved, but what most distressed me, he would neither take his eyes away from me nor look me fairly in the face. What he was, whether by trade or birth, was more than I could fathom. He seemed most like an old, unprofitable servingman.

"Are ye sharp-set?" he asked, glancing at about the level of my knee. "You can eat that drop parritch?" I said I feared it was his own supper. "O," said he, "I can do fine wanting it. I'll take the ale, though, for it moistens my cough." He drank the cup about half out and then suddenly held out his hand. "Let's see the letter." I told him the letter was for Mr. Balfour; not for him. "And who do ye think I am?" says he. "Give me Alexander's letter!"

"You know my father's name?"

"It would be strange if I didnae," he returned, "for he was my brother. And little as ye seem to like me, my house, or my good parritch, I'm your uncle. So give us the letter, Davie, my man, and sit down and fill your kyte."

What with shame, weariness, and disappointment, I could find no words, but handed him the letter, and sat down to the porridge with as little appetite as ever a young man had.

Meanwhile my uncle, stooping over the fire, turned the letter over and over in his hands. "Do ye ken what's in it?" he asked suddenly.

"You see for yourself, sir," said I, "that the seal has not been broken."

"Ay," said he, "but what brought you here? Ye'll have had some hopes, nae doubt?"

"I confess, sir," said I, "when I was told that I had kinsfolk well-to-do, I did hope that they might help me. But I am no beggar. I want no favors that are not freely given. For poor as I appear, I have friends that will be blithe to help me."

"Hoot-toot!" said Uncle Ebenezer. "Dinnae fly up at me. We'll agree fine yet. And, Davie, if you're done with that bit parritch, I could just take a sup of it myself." As soon as he had ousted me from the stool and spoon he murmured a little grace and fell to. "Your father was a hearty, if not a great eater; but as for me, I could never do mair than pyke at food." He took a pull at the beer. "If ye're dry, ye'll find water behind the door."

To this I returned no answer, standing stiffly on my two feet, and looking down upon my uncle with a mighty angry heart. He, on his part, continued to eat like a man under some pressure of time, and to throw out little darting glances at my shoes and stockings. Once only, our eyes met; and no thief taken with a hand in a man's pockets could have shown more lively signals of distress.

"Your father's been long dead?" he asked suddenly.

"Three weeks, sir," said I.

"He was a secret man, Alexander—a secret, silent man," he continued. "He never said muckle when he was young. He'll never have spoken muckle of me?"

"I never knew, sir, till you told me, that he had a brother."

"Dear me," said Ebenezer. "Nor yet of Shaws, I daresay?"

"Not so much as the name, sir," said I.

"To think o' that!" said he. "A strange nature of a man!" But for all that, he seemed singularly satisfied, though just why was more than I could read. Certainly, he seemed to be outgrowing the distaste that he had conceived against me; for presently he jumped up, came across the room behind me, and hit me a smack upon the shoulder.

"We'll agree fine yet!" he cried. "I'm just as glad I let you in. And now come awa' to bed."

To my surprise, he lit no lamp or candle, but groped his way, breathing deeply, up a dark flight of steps, and paused before a door, which he unlocked. He bade me go in, but I paused after a few steps, and begged a light.

"Hoot-toot!" said Uncle Ebenezer. "There's a fine moon."

"There's neither moon nor star, sir," said I. "I cannae see the bed."

"Hoot-toot!" said he. "Lights in a house is a thing I dinnae agree with. I'm unco feared of fires. Good night to ye, Davie, my man." And before I had time to add a further protest, he pulled the door to, and I heard him lock me in from outside.

I did not know whether to laugh or cry. The room was as cold as a well, and the bed, when I found my way to it, as damp as a peat bog. But, by good fortune, I had caught up my bundle and

9

my plaid, and rolling myself in the latter, I lay down upon the floor, and fell speedily asleep.

With the first peep of day I opened my eyes, to find myself in a great chamber, hung with stamped leather and furnished with fine embroidered furniture. Ten years ago it must have been as pleasant a room as a man could wish; but damp, dirt, disuse, and the mice and spiders had done their worst since then. Many of the windowpanes were broken; and indeed this was so common a feature in that house, that I believe my uncle must at some time have stood a siege from his indignant neighbors.

Meanwhile the sun was shining, so I knocked and shouted till my jailer let me out. He led me to the back of the house and a well, and told me to wash my face there, if I wanted. When that was done, I made my way back to the kitchen, where he had lit the fire and was making porridge. The table was laid with two bowls and two horn spoons, but the same single measure of beer. Perhaps my eye must have rested on this particular with some surprise, for my uncle spoke up as if in answer to my thought, asking me if I would like beer.

I told him not to put himself out. "Na, na," said he; "I'll deny you nothing in reason."

He fetched another cup, and then, to my great surprise, poured an accurate half from his cup to the other. There was a kind of nobleness in this that took my breath away. If my uncle was a miser, he was one of that thorough breed that goes near to make the vice respectable.

When we had made an end of our meal, my uncle unlocked a drawer and drew out of it a clay pipe and a lump of tobacco before he locked it up again. Then he sat down in the sun at one of the windows and silently smoked. From time to time his eyes came coasting round to me, and he shot out a question. Once it was, "And your mother?" and when I had told him that she, too, was dead, "Ay, she was a bonnie lassie!" Then, after another long pause, "Whae were these friends o' yours?"

I told him they were different gentlemen of the name of Campbell; though, indeed, there was only the minister that ever had taken the least note of me. But I began to think my uncle made too light of my position, and I did not wish him to suppose me helpless.

He seemed to turn this over in his mind; and then, "Davie, my man," said he, "ye've come to the right bit when ye came to your Uncle Ebenezer. I've a great notion of the family, and I mean to do the right by you. But while I'm thinking to mysel' of what's the best thing to put you to—the law, or the meenistry, or maybe the army—I wouldnae like the Balfours to be humbled before a few Campbells, and I'll ask you to keep your tongue within your teeth. No kind of word to onybody; or else—there's my door."

"Uncle Ebenezer," said I, "I've no manner of reason to suppose you mean anything but well of me. For all that, if you show me your door again, I'll take you at the word."

He seemed grievously put out. "Hoot-toots," said he, "just you give me a day or two, and say naething to naebody, and as sure as sure, I'll do the right by you."

"Very well," said I, "enough said." It seemed to me too soon, I daresay, that I was getting the upper hand of my uncle; and I began next to say that I must have my bed and bedclothes aired.

"Is this my house or yours?" said he in his keen voice, and then broke off, "Na, na, what's mine is yours, Davie, and what's yours is mine. Blood's thicker than water; and there's naebody but you and me that ought the name." And then on he rambled about the family and his father that began to enlarge the house, and himself that stopped the building as a sinful waste; and this put it in my head to give him Jennet Clouston's message.

"The hussy!" he cried. "Twelve hunner and nineteen—that's every day since I had her sold up! I'll have her roasted on red peats before I'm by with it! A witch—a proclaimed witch! I'll aff and see the session clerk."

And with that he unlocked a chest, and got out a very old and well-preserved blue coat and waistcoat, and a beaver hat. These he threw on and, taking a staff from the cupboard, was for setting out, when a thought arrested him. "I cannae leave you by yoursel' in the house," said he. "I'll have to lock you out."

The blood came to my face. "If you lock me out," I said, "it'll be the last you'll see of me in friendship."

He turned very pale, and sucked his mouth in. "This is no the way to win my favor, David."

"Sir," says I, "with a proper reverence for your age and our common blood, I do not value your favor at a bodle's purchase. If you were all the family I had in the world ten times over, I wouldn't buy your liking at such prices."

Uncle Ebenezer went and looked out of the window. I could see him trembling and twitching but when he turned round he had a smile upon his face. "Well," said he, "we must bear and forbear. I'll no go. That's all that's to be said of it."

"Uncle Ebenezer," I said, "I can make nothing out of this. You hate to have me in this house. You let me see it, every word and every minute. As for me, I've spoken to you as I never thought to speak to any man. Why do you seek to keep me, then? Let me gang back to my friends."

"Na, na," he said, very earnestly. "I like you fine and for the honor of the house I couldnae let you leave the way ye came. Bide here quiet and ye'll find that we agree."

"Well, sir," said I, after I had thought the matter out, "I'll stay awhile. It's more just I should be helped by my own blood than strangers. And if we don't agree, I'll do my best it shall be through no fault of mine."

That noon we had the porridge cold again. My uncle spoke but little, and when I sought to lead him to talk about my future, slipped out of it again. In a room next to the kitchen, where he suffered me to go, I found a great number of books in which I took great pleasure all afternoon.

One thing I discovered which put me in some doubt. This was an entry on the flyleaf of a book plainly written by my father's hand: *To my brother Ebenezer on his fifth birthday.* What puzzled me was this: That as my father was of course the younger brother, he must either have made some error, or he must have written before he was yet five in an excellent, manly hand.

When at length I went back to the kitchen, and sat down once

more to porridge and beer, the first thing I asked Uncle Ebenezer
was if my father had not been very quick at his books.

"Alexander? No him!" was the reply. "Why, I could read as
soon as he could."

This puzzled me yet more; and a thought coming into my head,
I asked if he and my father had been twins.

He jumped up and his horn spoon fell out of his hand upon the
floor. "Why do ye ask that?" he said, and he caught me by the
breast of the jacket. This time his little eyes, light and bright like
a bird's, looked straight into mine.

"What do you mean?" I asked, very calmly, for I was far
stronger than he, and not easily frightened. "Take your hand
from my jacket."

My uncle made a great effort upon himself. "David," he said,
"ye shouldnae speak to me about your father. That's the mistake."
He sat down and shook, blinking at his plate. "He was all the
brother that ever I had," he added, but with no heart in his voice.
Then he caught up his spoon and fell to supper again.

Now this laying of hands upon me and sudden profession of
love for my dead father went clean beyond my comprehension.
On the one hand, I began to think my uncle was perhaps insane;
on the other, there came to my mind a ballad I had heard of a poor
lad that was a rightful heir and a wicked kinsman that tried to
keep him from his own. For why should my uncle play a part
with a relative that came almost a beggar to his door unless, in
his heart, he had some cause to fear him?

With this notion getting firmly settled in my head, I now began
to imitate his covert looks; so that we sat silently at table like
a cat and mouse, each stealthily observing the other. He was busy
turning something over in his mind, and the longer we sat, the
more certain I became that the something was unfriendly to myself.

When he had cleared the platter, he got out his pipe, turned
round a stool into the chimney corner, and sat a while smoking,
with his back to me. "Davie," he said at length, "I've been thinking. There's a wee bit siller for ye that I half promised to your
father before ye were born. Naething legal, ye understand; just

13

gentlemen daffing at their wine. Well, that money has grown by now to be a matter of—" here he paused and stumbled "—of exactly forty pounds!" This he rapped out, and, with a sidelong glance over his shoulder, added, almost with a scream, "Scots!"

The Scots pound being worth no more than an English shilling, the difference made by this second thought was considerable. I could see, besides, that the whole story was a lie, invented with some puzzling end, and I made no attempt to conceal the tone of raillery in which I answered. "O, think again, sir! Pounds sterling, I believe!"

"That's what I said," returned my uncle. "Pounds sterling! And if you'll step out of the door, just to see what kind of a night it is, I'll get it out and call ye in again."

I did his will, smiling in my contempt that he should think I was so easily to be deceived. It was a dark night, with a few stars. I heard a hollow moaning of wind far off among the hills and I said to myself there was something thundery and changeful in the weather, little knowing what a vast importance that should prove to me before the evening passed.

When I was called in again, my uncle counted out seven and thirty golden guinea pieces. The rest was in his hand, in change, but his heart failed him, and he crammed it into his pocket. "There," said he, "I'm a queer man, and strange wi' strangers. But there's proof that my word is my bond."

Now, my uncle had seemed so miserly that I was struck dumb by this sudden generosity, and could find no words to thank him.

"I want nae thanks," said he. "I do my duty. I'm no saying that everybody would have done it, but for my part, it's a pleasure to do the right by my brother's son and to think that now we'll agree as such near friends should."

I thanked him as handsomely as I was able, all the while wondering why he had parted with his precious guineas.

Presently he looked towards me sideways. "And see here," says he, "tit for tat."

I told him I was ready to prove my gratitude in any reasonable degree, and then waited for some monstrous demand. And yet, when at last he spoke, it was only to tell me that he was growing old and a little broken, and that he would expect me to help him with the house. I expressed my readiness to serve.

"Well," he said, "let's begin." He pulled out of his pocket a rusty key. "There's the key of the stair tower," he says. "Ye can only get into it from the outside, for that part of the house is no finished. Gang ye up the stairs, and bring me down the chest that's at the top. There's papers in't."

"Can I have a light, sir?" said I.

"Na," said he, very cunningly. "Nae lights in my house. Just keep to the wall. There's nae bannisters. But the stairs are grand underfoot."

Out I went into the night. The wind was still moaning in the distance. It had fallen blacker than ever, and I felt along the wall till I came to the stair-tower door at the end of the unfinished wing. I had just turned the key in the keyhole when all upon a sudden, without a sound of thunder, the whole sky lighted up with wild fire and went black again. I was half blinded when I stepped into the tower.

It was so dark inside, it seemed a body could scarce breathe. I pushed out with hand and foot, and presently struck the wall with the one, and the lowermost round of the stair with the other. Minding my uncle's word about the bannister, I kept close to the tower side, and felt my way with a beating heart.

The house of Shaws stood five stories high. As I advanced, a second blink of summer lightning came and went. Fear had me by the throat and it was more by Heaven's mercy than my own strength that I did not fall. The flash not only shone in on every side through breaches in the wall, so that I seemed to be clambering aloft upon a scaffold, but it showed me the steps were of unequal length, and that one of my feet rested that moment within two inches of the well.

So this was the grand stair! A gust of angry courage came into my heart. My uncle had sent me here, certainly to run great risks, perhaps to die. I swore I would settle that "perhaps," if I should break my neck for it. I got down upon hands and knees, and as slowly as a snail, feeling before me every inch, I continued to ascend the stair. The darkness appeared to have redoubled and my mind was now confounded by a great stir of bats. Flying down from the top of the tower, the foul beasts beat about my face and body.

The tower, I should have said, was square. In every corner the step was made of a great stone to join the flights. Well, I had come close to one of these turns, when, feeling forward as usual, my hand slipped upon the edge and found nothing but emptiness. The stair had been carried no higher: to set a stranger mounting it in darkness was to send him to his death. Although, thanks to the lightning and my own precautions, I was safe, the mere thought of the peril in which I had stood brought out the sweat upon my body.

Knowing what I wanted now, I turned and groped my way down. Halfway, the wind sprang up in a clap, shook the tower, and died again. The rain followed in buckets. Reaching the ground level I looked towards the kitchen. The door stood open and shed a little glimmer of light. I could see my uncle standing in the rain, quite still, like a man hearkening.

Then there came a blinding flash and a great tow-row of thunder. Whether my uncle thought the crash to be the sound of my fall, or whether he heard in it God's voice denouncing murder, I will leave you to guess. Certain it is that he was seized by a kind of panic, and ran into the house and left the door open behind him. I followed as softly as I could and, coming unheard into the kitchen, stood and watched him.

He had found time to open the corner cupboard and bring out a great bottle of aqua vitae, and now sat with his back towards me at the table. Ever and again he would be seized with shuddering, and groan aloud, and carrying the bottle to his lips, drink down the raw spirits by the mouthful.

I came close behind him where he sat, and suddenly clapping my hands upon his shoulders, "Ah!" cried I.

My uncle gave a broken cry like a sheep's bleat, flung up his arms, and tumbled to the floor like a dead man. I was somewhat shocked at this, but the keys were hanging in the cupboard, and it was my design to arm myself before he should come to his senses and the power of devising evil. In the cupboard were a few medicine bottles and a great many papers, which I would willingly enough have rummaged, had I had the time.

I turned to the chests. The first was full of meal, the second of moneybags; but in the third, with many other things, I found a rusty, ugly-looking Highland dirk. This I concealed inside my waistcoat, and turned to my uncle.

He lay as he had fallen, all huddled. His face had a strange blue color and he seemed to have ceased breathing. Fear came on me that he was dead. I got water and dashed it in his face; and with that he seemed to come a little to himself, working his mouth and fluttering his eyelids. At last he looked up and saw me, and a terror came into his eyes.

"Are you alive?" he sobbed. "O man, are ye alive?"

"That am I," said I. "Small thanks to you!"

He had begun to seek for his breath with deep sighs. "The blue phial," said he, "in the corner cupboard—the blue phial." His breath came slower still.

I ran to the cupboard, and, sure enough, found there a blue phial of medicine. This I administered to him with what speed I might.

"It's the trouble," said he, reviving a little; "I have a trouble, Davie. It's the heart."

I set him on a chair and looked at him. It is true I felt some pity for a man that looked so sick, but I was full of righteous anger and I numbered over before him all the points of his behavior on which I wanted an explanation.

He heard me through in silence; and then, in a broken voice, begged me to let him go to bed.

"I'll tell ye the morn," he said; "as sure as death I will."

So weak was he that I could do nothing but consent. I locked him in his room, however, and pocketed the key. Then, returning to the kitchen, I made up a blaze and, wrapping myself in my plaid, lay down upon the chests and fell asleep.

CHAPTER III

What befell at the Queen's Ferry

NEXT MORNING THERE BLEW a bitter wintry wind out of the north-west, driving scattered rain clouds. For all that, I made my way to the side of a nearby burn and had a plunge. All aglow from my bath, I sat down once more beside the fire and began gravely to consider my position.

There was now no doubt I carried my life in my hand, and my uncle would leave no stone unturned that he might compass my destruction. But I was young and spirited, and like most country-bred lads, I had a great opinion of my shrewdness. I had come to his door little more than a child and he had met me with treachery and violence. It would be a fine consummation to take the upper hand and drive him like a sheep.

I sat there smiling at the fire, and I saw myself in fancy grow to be his ruler. But in all the shapes and pictures that I gazed at in the burning coal, there was never the least sign of all those tribulations that were ripe to fall on me.

Presently, swollen with conceit, I went upstairs and gave my prisoner his liberty. We bade each other good morning civilly and soon we were set to breakfast, as it might have been the day before.

"Well, sir," said I, with a jeering tone, "it will be time, I think, to understand each other. You took me for a country Johnnie Raw, with no more wit or courage than a porridge stick. I took you for a good man, or no worse than others at the least. We were both wrong. What cause have you to cheat me, and attempt my life?"

He murmured something about a jest, and that he liked a bit of fun; then, seeing me smile, assured me he would make all clear as soon as he had breakfasted. I saw by his face that he had no lie ready for me and I was about to tell him so, when we were interrupted by a knocking at the door.

I went to open it and found on the doorstep a half-grown boy in sea clothes. He had no sooner seen me than he had begun to dance some steps of the sea hornpipe, snapping his fingers in the air. For all that, he was blue with the cold, and there was a pathetic look in his face that consisted ill with this gaiety.

"What cheer, mate?" says he, with a cracked voice.

I asked him soberly to name his pleasure, and he began to sing. "Well," said I, "if you have no business at all, I will be so unmannerly as to shut you out."

"Stay, brother!" he cried. "Have you no fun about you? Or do you want to get me thrashed? I've brought a letter from old Heasyoasy to Mr. Belflower." He showed me a letter. "And I say, mate, I'm mortal hungry."

"Well," said I, "you shall have a bite if I go empty for it."

With that I brought him in and set him down to my own place, where he fell to greedily on the remains of breakfast. Meanwhile, my uncle read the letter and sat thinking; then, suddenly, he got to his feet with a great liveliness, and pulled me into the farthest corner of the room.

"Davie," said he, "I have a venture with one Hoseason, the captain of a trading brig, the *Covenant*, of Dysart, which sails today for overseas. Now, if you and me was to walk over with yon lad to the Queen's Ferry, I could see the captain at the Hawes Inn, or maybe on board the *Covenant* if there was papers to be signed. So far from a loss of time, we can jog on to my agent and lawyer, Mr. Rankeillor. After a' that's come and gone, ye would be unwilling to believe my naked word. But ye'll believe Rankeillor. He's factor to half the gentry in these parts; an auld, highly respeckit man, who kenned your father."

I thought awhile. I was going to some doubtless populous place of shipping, where my uncle durst attempt no violence, and, once there, I could force on the visit to the lawyer even if my uncle were now insincere in proposing it. "Very well," says I, "let us go to the Ferry."

My uncle got into his hat and coat, and buckled an old rusty cutlass on. Then we trod the fire out, locked the door, and set forth upon our walk.

The cold northwest wind blew in our faces. The grass was all white with June daisies and the trees with blossom; but, to judge by our blue nails and aching wrists, the whiteness might have been a winter frost. Uncle Ebenezer trudged in the ditch, jogging from side to side like an old ploughman. He never said a word and I was thrown for talk on the cabin boy. He told me his name was Ransome, and that he had followed the sea since he was nine, but could not say how old he was, as he had lost his reckoning.

I asked him of the brig (which he declared was the finest ship that sailed) and of her captain, in whose praises he was equally loud. Hoseason was a man, by his account, that would "crack on all sail into the day of judgment"; fierce, unscrupulous and brutal. All this my poor cabin boy had taught himself to admire as seaman-like and manly. He would only admit one flaw in his idol. "He ain't no seaman," he admitted. "Mr. Shuan navigates the brig, and he's the finest seaman in the trade, only for drink. Why, look 'ere"; and turning down his stocking he showed me a raw wound that made my blood run cold. "Mr. Shuan done that," he said, with an air of pride.

"What!" I cried. "Do you take such savage usage at his hands? Why, you are no slave, to be so handled!"

"No," said Ransome, changing his tune at once, "and so he'll find. See 'ere"; and he showed me a great knife, which he told me was stolen. "I'll do for him! O, he ain't the first!"

It began to come over me that the *Covenant* (for all her pious name) was little better than a hell upon the seas. "In Heaven's name," cried I, "can you find no reputable life on shore?"

"O, no, it's not as bad as that," said he. "There's worse off than me: there's the twenty-pounders. O, laws! You should see them being taken on board!" It came in on me he meant those unhappy criminals who were sent overseas to slavery in North America, or the still more unhappy innocents who were kidnapped (or trepanned, as the word went) for private interest or vengeance.

Just then we came to the top of the hill, and looked down on the Ferry. The Firth of Forth narrows at this point to the width of a good-sized river, which makes a convenient place for a ferry, and turns the upper reach beyond the town of Queensferry into a landlocked haven for ships. On the south shore they have built a pier for the Ferry and, at the land end of the pier, on the other side of the road, and backed against a pretty garden of holly trees and hawthorns, I could see the Hawes Inn.

The neighborhood of the inn looked pretty lonely, for the boat had just gone north with passengers. A skiff, however, lay beside the pier, with some seamen sleeping on the thwarts. This, as Ransome told me, was the brig's boat waiting for the captain; and about half a mile off, alone in the anchorage, was the *Covenant* herself. There was a seagoing bustle on board; yards were swinging into place and I could hear the sailors' song as they pulled upon the ropes.

After all I had listened to upon the way, I looked at that ship with extreme abhorrence, and now, as we all three pulled up on the brow of the hill, I addressed my uncle. "I think it right to tell you, sir," says I, "that nothing will bring me on board that *Covenant*."

He seemed to waken from a dream. "Eh?" he said. "Well, well, we'll have to please ye, I suppose. But what are we standing here for? It's perishing cold; and if I'm no mistaken, they're busking the *Covenant* for sea."

As soon as we came to the inn, Ransome led us up the stair to a small room, heated like an oven by a great coal fire. At a table by the chimney, a tall, dark, sober-looking man sat writing. In spite of the heat of the room, he wore a thick sea jacket, buttoned to the neck, and a hairy cap drawn down over his ears. Yet looking cool and self-possessed, he got to his feet at once and offered his large hand to Ebenezer. "I am glad that ye are here in time, Mr. Balfour," said he, in a fine deep voice. "The wind's fair, and the tide upon the turn. We'll sail before tonight."

"Captain Hoseason," returned my uncle, "you keep your room unco hot."

"It's a habit I have, Mr. Balfour," said the skipper. "I have a cold blood, sir. There's neither fur nor flannel—no, sir, nor hot rum—will warm the temperature. It's the same with most men that have been in the tropic seas."

Now this fancy of the captain's had a great share in my misfortunes. For though I had promised myself not to let my kinsman out of sight, I was both so impatient for a nearer look of the sea (you are to remember I had lived all my life in the inland hills), and so sickened by the closeness of the room, that when he told me to "run downstairs and play myself awhile," I was fool enough to take him at his word.

Away I went, leaving the two men sitting down to a bottle and a great mass of papers, and crossing the road in front of the inn, walked down upon the beach. Little wavelets, not much bigger than I had seen upon a lake, beat upon the shore. But the weeds were new to me—some green, some brown and long, and some with little bladders that cracked between my fingers. Even so far up the firth, the smell of the seawater was exceedingly salt and stirring, and the spirit of all that I beheld put me in thoughts of far voyages and foreign places. I looked at the seamen with the skiff—big brown fellows, some with colored handkerchiefs about their throats, one with a brace of pistols stuck into his pockets, two or three with knotty bludgeons, and all with knives. I passed the time of day with one that looked less desperate than his fellows, and asked him of the sailing of the brig. He said they would get under way as soon as the ebb set, but he expressed himself with such horrifying oaths that I made haste to get away from him.

This threw me back on Ransome, who came out of the inn and ran to me, crying for a bowl of punch. I told him neither he nor I was of an age for such indulgences. "But a glass of ale you may have, and welcome," said I. He mopped and mowed at me, but he was glad to get the ale, and presently we were set down in the front room of the inn, eating and drinking with a good appetite.

Here it occurred to me that, as the landlord was a man of that country, I might do well to make a friend of him, and I asked him whether he knew Mr. Rankeillor.

"Ay, a very honest man," says he. "And, by the by, was it you that came in with Ebenezer?" And when I had told him yes, "Ye'll be no relative of his?" he asked. I told him no, none. "I thought not," said he, "and yet ye have a kind of look of Mr. Alexander."

I said it seemed that Ebenezer was ill-seen in the country.

"Nae doubt," said the landlord. "There's many would like to see him girning on a rope: Jennet Clouston and mony mair that he has harried out of house and hame. And yet he was ance a fine young fellow, too. But that was before the report gaed abroad about Mr. Alexander."

"And what was it?" I asked.

"Ou, just that he had killed him," said the landlord. "Did ye never hear that?"

"And what would he kill him for?" said I.

"What for, but to get The Shaws," said he.

"Is that so?" said I. "Was my—was Alexander the eldest son?"

"'Deed was he," said the landlord. "What else would he have killed him for?" And with that he went away.

Of course, I had guessed it a long while ago; but it is one thing to guess, another to know. I sat stunned with my good fortune, and could scarce believe that the same poor lad who had trudged in the dust from Essendean not two days ago was now one of the rich of the earth, and might mount his horse tomorrow. All these pleasant things crowded into my mind as I sat staring before me out of the inn window, and paying no heed to what I saw; only I remember that my eye lighted on Captain Hoseason down on the pier among his seamen. Presently he came marching back towards the house, carrying his tall figure with a manly bearing, and still with the same sober, grave expression on his face. I wondered if it was possible that any of Ransome's stories could be true; they all fitted so ill with the man's looks.

The next thing, I heard my uncle calling me, and found the pair in the road together. "Sir," said the captain, with an air (very flattering to a young lad) of grave equality, "Mr. Balfour tells me great things of you. I wish I was longer here that we might make the better friends. But come on board my brig for half an hour, till the ebb sets, and drink a bowl with me."

Now, I longed to see the inside of a ship; but I was not going to put myself in jeopardy, and I told him my uncle and I had an appointment with a lawyer.

"Ay, ay," said the captain, "he passed me word of that. But the boat'll set ye ashore at the town pier, and that's but a stone-cast from Rankeillor's house." And he suddenly leaned down and whispered in my ear: "Take care of the old fox. He means mischief. Come aboard till I can get a word with ye."

And then, passing his arm through mine, he continued aloud, as he set off towards his boat: "But come, what can I bring ye from the Carolinas? Any friend of Mr. Balfour's can command. A roll of tobacco? Indian featherwork? A stone pipe? The mocking-bird that mews for all the world like a cat? Say your pleasure."

By this time we were at the boatside, and he was handing me in. I did not dream of hanging back; I thought (the poor fool!) that I had found a good friend and helper, and I was rejoiced to see the ship. As soon as we were all set in our places, the boat thrust off from the pier and began to move over the waters; and what with my pleasure in this new movement and my surprise at the grow-ing bigness of the brig as we drew near to it, I hardly under-stood what the captain said.

As soon as we were alongside (where I sat fairly gaping at the ship's height), Hoseason, declaring that he and I must be the first aboard, ordered a tackle to be sent down from the main yard. In this I was whipped into the air and set down again on the deck, where the captain stood waiting for me, and instantly slipped back his arm under mine. There I stood some while, a little dizzy, while the captain pointed out the strange sights around me.

"But where is my uncle?" said I, suddenly.

"Ay," said Hoseason, with a sudden grimness, "that's the point."

I felt I was lost. With all my strength I plucked myself clear of him, and ran to the bulwarks. Sure enough, there was the boat pulling for the town, with my uncle in the stern. I gave a piercing cry—"Help, help! Murder!"—so that both sides of the anchorage rang with it, and my uncle turned round and showed me a face full of cruelty and terror.

It was the last I saw. Already strong hands had been plucking me back from the side. Now a thunderbolt seemed to strike me. I saw a flash of fire, and fell senseless.

CHAPTER IV

I go to sea in the brig "Covenant" of Dysart

I CAME TO MYSELF IN DARKNESS, bound hand and foot. There sounded in my ears the thrashing of heavy sprays, the thundering of the sails, and the shrill cries of seamen. The whole world heaved giddily up and down. So sick and hurt was I that it took me a long while, chasing my thoughts and ever stunned by a fresh stab of pain, to realize that I must be lying somewhere in the belly of the *Covenant*, and that the wind must have strengthened to a gale. With the clear perception of my plight, there fell upon me remorse at my own folly and a passion of anger at my uncle.

During these first hours aboard the brig I had no measure of time. Day and night were alike in that ill-smelling cavern, and the misery of my situation drew out the hours to double while I lay waiting to hear the ship split upon some rock or to feel her reel head foremost into the depths of the sea. But sleep at length stole from me the consciousness of sorrow.

I was wakened by the light of a lantern shining in my face. A small man of about thirty, with green eyes and a tangle of fair hair, stood looking down at me. "Well," said he, "how goes it?"

I answered by a sob, and my visitor then felt my pulse and set himself to wash and dress the wound upon my scalp. "Ay," said he, "cheer up! The world's no done. Have you had any meat?"

I said I could not look at it, and thereupon he gave me some brandy and water in a tin pannikin, and left me once more to myself. The next time he came, I was lying betwixt sleep and waking, the sickness succeeded by a horrid giddiness. I ached in every limb, and the cords that bound me seemed to be of fire. I had suffered tortures of fear, now from the ship's rats that sometimes pattered on my face, and now from the dismal imaginings that haunt the bed of fever.

The glimmer of the lantern, as a trap opened, shone in like the heaven's sunlight. The man with the green eyes descended the ladder somewhat unsteadily. He was followed by the captain. Neither said a word; but the first examined me and dressed my wound as before, while Hoseason looked me in my face with an odd, black look.

"Now, sir, you see for yourself," said the first; "a high fever and no appetite. I want the boy taken out of this hole and put in the forecastle."

"What ye may want, Mr. Riach, is a matter of concern to nobody but yoursel'," returned the captain; "but I can tell ye that which is to be. Here he is; here he shall bide."

"I will crave leave humbly to say that I am paid, and none too much, to be the second officer of this old tub," said the other. "But I am paid for nothing more. Admitting that you have been paid to do a murder—"

Hoseason turned upon him with a flash. "What kind of talk is that?" he cried. "I have sailed with ye three cruises. In all that time, sir, ye should have learned to know me. I'm a stiff man, but if ye say the lad will die—"

"Ay, will he!" said Mr. Riach.

"Well, sir, is not that enough?" said Hoseason. "Flit him where ye please!"

Thereupon the captain ascended the ladder. Mr. Riach turned after him and bowed low in what was plainly a spirit of derision. Even in my state of sickness, I perceived that the mate was touched with liquor and that, drunk or sober, he was like to prove a valuable friend.

Five minutes afterwards my bonds were cut, I was carried up to the forecastle, and laid in a bunk where it was a blessed thing to open my eyes again upon daylight. The forecastle was a roomy place enough, set about with berths, in which men were seated smoking, or lying down asleep. The day being calm and the wind fair, the hatchway was open and, as the ship rolled, a dusty beam of sunlight shone in. One of the men brought me a healing drink which Mr. Riach had prepared, and bade me lie still and I should soon be well again. There were no bones broken, he explained: "The blow on the head was naething. It was me that gave it ye!"

Here I lay, a prisoner, for many days, and not only got my health again, but came to know my companions. They were a rough lot indeed, being men rooted out of all the kindly parts of life. Some had sailed with the pirates, some had run from the King's ships; and all, as the saying goes, were "at a word and a blow" with their best friends. Yet I had not been many days with them before I began to be ashamed of my first judgment of them. No class of man is altogether bad, and these shipmates were no exception. Among their good deeds, they returned my money, which had been shared among them. Though it was about a third short, I was very glad to get it, and hoped great good from it in the Carolinas (in those days of my youth, white men were still sold into slavery on the plantations), for that was the destiny to which my wicked uncle had condemned me.

Ransome came in at times from the roundhouse, where he berthed and served, now nursing a bruised limb in silent agony, now raving against the cruelty of Mr. Shuan. It made my heart bleed, but the men had a great respect for the chief mate, who was, as they said, "the only seaman of the whole jing-bang, and none such a bad man when he was sober." Indeed, I found there was a strange peculiarity about our two mates. Mr. Riach was sullen, unkind, and harsh when he was sober; Mr. Shuan would not hurt a fly except when he was drinking. It was Mr. Riach (Heaven forgive him!) who gave drink to Ransome, and it was, doubtless, kindly meant; but it was the pitifullest thing to see the unhappy boy staggering, dancing, and talking he knew not what.

All this time, the *Covenant* was tumbling up and down against head seas, so that the hatchway was almost constantly shut, and the forecastle lighted only by a swinging lantern. There was constant labor for all hands. The sails had to be made and shortened every hour. The strain told on the men's temper and there was a growl of quarreling all day long from berth to berth. As I was never allowed to set my foot on deck, you can picture how weary of my life I grew to be.

Then, one night, about eleven o'clock, a man on watch came below for his jacket. Instantly there began to go a whisper about the forecastle that "Shuan had done for him at last." We all knew who was meant—but we had scarce time to get the idea rightly in our heads when the hatchway was flung open, and Captain Hoseason came down the ladder. He looked sharply round the bunks in the tossing light of the lantern; and then, walking straight up to me, he addressed me, to my surprise, in tones of kindness. "My man, we want ye to serve in the roundhouse. You and Ransome are to change berths. Run away aft with ye."

As he spoke, two seamen appeared in the hatchway carrying Ransome in their arms. The ship gave a great sheer and the light of the swinging lantern fell direct on the boy's face. It was as white as wax and had a dreadful smile. The blood in me ran cold, and I drew in my breath as if I had been struck.

"Run away aft!" cried Hoseason. At that I brushed by the sailors and the boy (who neither spoke nor moved), and ran up on deck.

The brig was sheering giddily through a long cresting swell. Under the arched foot of the foresail, I could still see the sunset. This, at such an hour of the night, surprised me greatly, but I was too ignorant to draw the conclusion—that we were going north-about round Scotland and were now between the Orkney and Shetland Islands. For my part, who had been so long shut in the dark and knew nothing of head winds, I thought we might be halfway across the Atlantic. I pushed on across the decks, running between the seas, catching at ropes, and was only saved from going overboard by one of the hands.

The roundhouse, where I was now to sleep and serve, stood some six feet above the decks, and was of good dimensions. Inside were a fixed table and bench, and two berths, one for the captain and the other for the two mates, turn and turn about. From top to bottom it was fitted with lockers for the officers' belongings and part of the ship's stores. Indeed, the best of the meat and drink and all the powder were there; and some of the cutlasses and all the firearms except the two pieces of brass ordnance were set in a rack in the roundhouse wall.

A small window and a skylight gave it light by day. When I entered, a lamp was burning, not brightly, but enough to show Mr.

Shuan sitting at the table with a brandy bottle in front of him. A tall, strongly made man, he took no notice of my coming in; nor did he move when the captain followed and leaned on the berth beside me, looking sternly at the mate. I stood in fear of Hoseason, but something told me I need not be afraid of him just then. I whispered in his ear: "How is he?" He shook his head like one that does not know and does not wish to think.

Presently Mr. Riach came in. He gave the captain a glance that meant the boy was dead as plain as speaking. All three of us stood without a word, staring down at Mr. Shuan, who all of a sudden put out his hand to take the bottle. At that Mr. Riach started forward, caught the bottle and tossed it through the door into the sea.

Mr. Shuan was on his feet in a trice: he would have done murder for the second time that night had not the captain stepped between him and the victim. "Sit down!" roars Hoseason. "Ye sot and swine, do ye know ye've murdered the boy!"

Mr. Shuan sat down again, and put his hand to his brow. "Well," he said, "he brought me a dirty pannikin!"

At that the captain, Mr. Riach, and I looked at each other for a second with a kind of fright. Then Hoseason took his chief officer by the shoulder, led him across to his bunk, and bade him lie down, as you might speak to a bad child. The murderer cried a little, but he took off his seaboots and obeyed.

"Ah!" cried Mr. Riach. "Ye should have interfered long syne."

"Mr. Riach," said Hoseason, "this night's work must never be kennt in Dysart. The boy went overboard, sir. That's the story, and I would give five pounds it was true!" He turned to the table. "What made ye throw the good bottle away? There was nae sense in that. Here, David, draw me another. They're in the bottom locker." He tossed me a key. "Ye'll need a glass yourself, sir," he added to Riach.

So the pair sat down and hob-a-nobbed, and in the course of that first night and the next day, I had got well into the run of my new duties. I had to serve at the meals, and all the day I would be running with a dram to one or the other of my three masters. At night I slept on a blanket thrown on the hard and cold deck boards of the roundhouse; nor was I suffered to sleep without interruption. When a fresh watch was to be set, two and sometimes all three would sit down and brew a bowl together. How they kept their health, I know not, any more than how I kept my own.

Yet in other ways it was an easy service. There was no cloth to lay; the meals were either of oatmeal porridge or salt beef, except twice a week when there was pudding. I was as well fed as the rest, and was even allowed my share of their pickles, which were the great dainty. Not being firm on my sea legs, I was clumsy and sometimes fell with what I was bringing them, but both Mr. Riach and the captain were singularly patient. Mr. Riach spoke to me like a friend when he was not sulking, and even the captain would sometimes unbuckle a bit and tell me of the fine countries he had visited. As for Mr. Shuan, the drink, or his crime, had certainly troubled his mind. He never grew used to my being there, stared at me continually (sometimes, I thought, with terror), and more than once drew back from my hand when I was serving him.

The shadow of poor Ransome, to be sure, lay on all four of us. And then I had my own trouble as well. I was doing dirty work for three men that I looked down upon, one of whom should have hung from the gallows. As for the future, I could only see myself slaving alongside Negroes in the tobacco fields. So, as the days came and went, my heart sank lower and lower, till I was even glad of the work which kept me from thinking.

CHAPTER V

The man with the belt of gold and the siege of the roundhouse

MORE THAN A WEEK WENT BY, in which the ill luck that had begun to pursue the *Covenant* grew yet more strongly marked. Some days she made a little way; others, she was actually driven back. At last we were beaten so far to the south that we tacked to and fro a whole day within sight of the wild, rocky coast of Cape Wrath. There followed a council of the officers, and some decision which

I did not rightly understand, seeing only that we had made a fair wind of a foul one and were now running south into The Minch.

The next afternoon there was a falling swell and a thick, wet fog that hid one end of the brig from the other. All afternoon, when I went on deck, I saw men listening hard over the bulwarks—"for breakers," they said. Though I did not understand the word, I felt danger in the air, and was excited.

Maybe about ten at night, I was serving Mr. Riach and the captain their supper, when the ship struck something with a great sound. My two masters leaped to their feet.

"She's struck!" said Mr. Riach.

"No, sir," said the captain. "We've only run a boat down." And they hurried out.

The captain was right. We had run down a boat in the fog, and she had gone to the bottom with all aboard but one. This man had been sitting in the stern as a passenger while the crew were on the benches rowing. At the moment of the blow, the stern had been thrown into the air, and the man had leaped up and caught hold of the brig's bowsprit. He had luck and much agility and unusual strength to have saved himself thus from such a pass. And yet, when the captain brought him into the roundhouse, he looked as cool as I did.

He was smallish but well set and nimble. His face was of a good open expression, sunburnt, heavily freckled and pitted with small-pox, and his unusually light eyes had a kind of dancing madness in them. When he took off his greatcoat, he laid a pair of fine silver-mounted pistols on the table, and I saw that he was belted with a great sword. With a feathered hat, a red waistcoat, breeches of black plush, and a blue coat with silver buttons and handsome silver lace, he showed forth mighty fine for the roundhouse of a merchant brig. His manners, besides, were elegant, and he pledged the captain handsomely.

"I'm vexed, sir, about the boat," replies the captain.

"There are some pretty men gone to the bottom," said the stranger, "that I would rather see on the dry land again than a score of boats. They would have died for me like dogs."

"Well, sir," said the captain, still watching him, "there are more men in the world than boats to put them in."

"Ye seem to be a gentleman of penetration," cried the other.

"I have been in France, sir," says the captain, so that it was plain he meant more by the words than showed upon the face of them.

"And so has many a pretty man, for the matter of that," says the other.

"No doubt, sir," says the captain, "and fine coats."

"Oho!" says the stranger. "Is that how the wind sets?" And he laid his hand quickly on his pistols.

"Don't be hasty," said Hoseason. "Ye've a French soldier's coat upon your back and a Scotch tongue in your head, to be sure, but so has many an honest fellow in these days."

"So," said the stranger, "are ye of the honest party?" (meaning, Was he a Jacobite? For each side, in these civil broils, takes the name of honesty for its own.)

"Why, sir," replied Hoseason, "I am a true-blue Protestant. But for all that, I can be sorry to see another man with his back to the wall."

"Can ye so, indeed?" asked the Jacobite. "Well, sir, to be plain with ye, if I got into the hands of any of the red-coated gentry, it would go hard with me. Now, sir, I was bound for France. There was a French ship cruising here to pick me up, but she gave us the go-by in the fog—as I wish that ye had done yoursel'! The best that I can say is this: if ye can set me ashore where I was going, I have that upon me will reward you highly for your trouble."

"In France?" says the captain. "No, sir; that I cannot do. But where ye come from—we might talk of that." And then, unhappily, he observed me standing in my corner, and packed me off to the galley to get supper for the gentleman. When I came back, I found the gentleman had taken a money belt from his waist, and poured a guinea or two upon the table. The captain was looking at the guineas, then at the belt, then at the gentleman's face. I thought he seemed excited. "Half of it," he cried, "and I'm your man!"

The other swept back the guineas into the belt, and put it on again under his waistcoat. "I have told ye, sir," said he, "that not one doit of it belongs to me. It belongs to my chieftain, and while I would be silly to grudge some of it that the rest might come safe, I should show myself a hound if I bought my own carcass too dear. Thirty guineas on the seaside, or sixty if ye set me on the Linnhe Loch. Take it, if ye will. If not, ye can do your worst."

"And if I give ye to the soldiers?" asked Hoseason.

"Ye would make a fool's bargain," said the other. "My chief's estate is in the hands of the man they call King George. It is his officers that collect the rents. But, for the honor of Scotland, the poor tenants take a thought upon their exiled chief, and this money is a part of that very rent for which King George is looking. Now, sir, bring it within Government's reach and how much of it'll come to you?"

"Little enough, to be sure," said Hoseason; and then, "Well, what must be must. Sixty guineas, and done. Here's my hand upon it."

"And here's mine," said the other.

And thereupon the captain went out (rather hurriedly, I thought), and left me alone in the roundhouse with the stranger. I had, of course, heard tell that at that period (so soon after the Scottish rebellion of 'Forty-five) there were many exiled Highland gentlemen coming back to Scotland at the peril of their lives. Now I had such a rebel under my eyes, who not only was a smuggler of rents, but had taken service with King Louis of France. And as if this were not enough, he had a belt full of golden guineas.

"And so you're a Jacobite?" said I with a lively interest, as I set meat before him.

"Ay," said he, beginning to eat. "And you, by your long face, should be a Whig?"

"Betwixt and between," said I, not to annoy him; although I was indeed a Whig and as loyal to King George as Mr. Campbell could make me.

"And that's naething," said he. "But this bottle of yours, Mr. Betwixt-and-Between, is dry. It's hard to pay sixty guineas and be grudged a dram."

"I'll go and ask for the key," said I, and stepped on deck.

The fog was close as ever, but the swell almost down. They had laid the brig to, not knowing precisely where they were. The captain and the two officers were in the waist with their heads together. It struck me (I don't know why) that they were after no good.

As I drew softly near, Mr. Riach's words more than confirmed me. "Couldn't we wile him out of the roundhouse?"

"He's better where he is," returned Hoseason; "he hasn't room to use his sword. We can get the man in talk, one upon each side, and pin him by the two arms."

Hearing this, I was seized with fear and anger at these treacherous, greedy men. My first mind was to run away. My second was bolder. "Captain," said I, "the gentleman is seeking a dram, and the bottle's out. Will you give me the key?"

They all started and turned about.

"Why, here's our chance to get the firearms!" Riach cried. "Do ye ken where the pistols are, David?"

"Ay, ay," put in Hoseason. "David kens, David's a good lad. Ye see, David my man, yon wild Hielandman is a danger to the ship, besides being a rank foe to King George."

I had never been so be-Davided since I came on board; but I said yes, as if all I heard were quite natural.

"The trouble is that all our firelocks and powder are in the roundhouse," resumed Hoseason. "Now, if one of us was to go in and take them, he would fall to thinking. But a lad like you, David, might snap up a horn and a pistol or two without remark. And if ye can do it cleverly, I'll bear it in mind when we come to Carolina. And yon man has a belt full of gold, that I give you my word you shall have your fingers in."

Though I had scarce breath to speak, I told him I would do as he wished, and upon that he gave me the key of the spirit locker, and I began to go slowly back to the roundhouse. What was I to do? They were dogs and thieves. They had stolen me from my country and had killed poor Ransome. Was I to hold the candle to another murder? But then, there was the fear of death very plain before me. What could a boy and a man do against a whole ship's company?

34

I was still arguing it back and forth when I came into the round-house and saw the Jacobite eating his supper under the lamp. At that, my mind was made up all in a moment. As if by compulsion, I put my hand on his shoulder. "Do ye want to be killed?" said I. He sprang to his feet, and looked a question at me as clear as if he had spoken. "They're all murderers here," I cried. "They've murdered a boy already. Now it's you."

"Ay, ay," said he; "but they haven't got me yet." And then, looking at me curiously, "Will ye stand with me?"

"That will I!" said I. "I'll stand by you."

"Why, then," said he, "what's your name?"

"David Balfour," said I; then thinking that a man with so fine a coat must like fine people, I added for the first time, "of Shaws."

It never occurred to him to doubt me, for a Highlander is used to see gentlefolks in poverty. But having no estate of his own, my words nettled a childish vanity he had. "My name is Stewart," he said, drawing himself up. "Alan Breck, they call me. A king's name is good enough for me, though I have the name of no big family to clap to the hind end of it."

And having administered this rebuke, he turned to examine our defenses. Of the apertures in the roundhouse, only the skylight and two stout oak doors were large enough for the passage of a man. I secured one door, but when I was proceeding to shut the other, Alan stopped me.

"David," said he "—for I cannae bring to mind the name of your landed estate, and so will make so bold as to call you David— that door is the best part of my defenses."

"It would be yet better shut," says I.

"Not so," says he. "As long as it is open and my face to it, my enemies will be in front of me."

He drew his great sword and made trial of the room he had to wield it in. Then he gave me from the rack a cutlass, choosing it with great care, shaking his head and saying he had never in all his life seen poorer weapons. Next he set me down to the table with a powder horn, a bag of bullets, and all the pistols which he bade me charge. "And now," said he, "do you give heed o' me?"

I told him I would listen closely.

"First of all," said he, "how many are against us?"

I reckoned them up. My chest was tight, my mouth dry, and such was my hurried mind I had to cast the numbers twice. "Fifteen," said I.

Alan whistled. "Well," said he, "that can't be cured. And now, give heed. It is my part to keep this door, where I look for the main battle. Dinnae fire to this side unless they get me down. I would rather have ten foes in front of me than one friend like you cracking pistols at my back." I told him, indeed I was no great shot. "And that's very bravely said," he cried. "There's many a gentleman that wouldnae dare to say it."

"But then, sir," said I, "they may break the door behind you."

"Ay," says he, "and that is a part of your work. Ye must climb up into yon bed where ye're handy at the window, and if they lift hand against the door, ye're to shoot. Let's make a bit of a soldier of ye, David. What else have ye to guard?"

"There's the skylight," said I. "But I would need eyes upon both sides to keep the two of them."

"That's very true," said Alan. "But have ye no ears?"

"To be sure!" cried I. "I must hear the bursting of the glass!"

"Ye have some rudiments of sense," said Alan grimly; and scarce had he spoken these words when the captain showed face in the open door.

"Stand!" cried Alan, and pointed his sword at him.

The captain neither winced nor drew back a foot. "A naked sword?" says he. "This is a strange return for hospitality."

"Do you see me?" asked Alan. "I come of kings; I bear a king's name. Do ye see my sword? It has slashed the heads off mair Whigamores than you have toes upon your feet. Call up your vermin, sir, and fall on!"

The captain said nothing to Alan, but he gave me an ugly look. "David," said he, "I'll mind this." Next moment he was gone.

"And now," said Alan, "the grip is coming." He drew a dirk, which he held in his left hand in case they should run in under his sword. I clambered up into the berth with an armful of pistols and set open the window. It was a small part of the deck that I could overlook, but enough. The sea had gone down and there was a great stillness in the ship, in which I heard the muttering of voices. A little after, there came a clash of steel upon the deck. I knew they were dealing out the cutlasses and one had been let fall: after that, silence again.

My heart beat like a bird's, both quick and little. I tried to pray, I remember, but the hurry of my mind, like a man running, would not suffer me to think upon the words. My chief wish was to have the thing begin and be done with it.

It came all of a sudden, with a rush of feet and a roar, then a shout from Alan, a sound of blows and someone crying out as if hurt. I looked back and saw Mr. Shuan in the doorway, crossing blades with Alan. "That's him that killed the boy!" I cried.

"Look to your window!" said Alan. As I turned I saw him pass his sword through the mate's body. My head was scarce back at the window, before five men, carrying an extra spar for a battering ram, took post to drive the door in. I had never fired with a pistol in my life but it was now or never. Just as they swung the spar I shot into their midst.

I hit one of them (it looked like the captain), for he sang out and gave back a step. The rest stopped, and before they had time to recover, I sent another ball over their heads, at which they threw down the yard and ran for it.

Then I looked round again. The whole deckhouse was full of the smoke of my firing. But there was Alan, standing as before; only now his sword was running blood to the hilt. Mr. Shuan, on hands and knees and with blood pouring from his mouth, was sinking slowly to the floor, and just as I looked, some of those from behind caught hold of him by the heels and dragged him out of the roundhouse.

"There's one of your Whigs for ye!" cried Alan.

I told him I thought I had winged the captain.

"And I've settled two," says he. "But, to your watch, David. This is but a dram before meat."

I settled back to recharge the pistols I had fired. Our enemies

37

were disputing not far off upon the deck, so loudly that I could hear a word or two. "It was Shuan bungled it," I heard one say.

Another answered, "Wheesht, man! He's paid the piper."

After that the voices fell into muttering. One person spoke as though laying down a plan. First one and then another answered him briefly, like men taking orders. I told Alan they must be coming on again.

"It's what we have to pray for," said he. "Or there'll be nae sleep for you or me. But this time, they'll be in earnest."

While the brush had lasted, I had not the time to think if I was frighted; but now, when all was still again, my mind ran upon nothing but the sharp swords and the cold steel. Presently, when I began to hear stealthy steps and a brushing of men's clothes against the roundhouse wall, and knew they were taking their places, I could have cried out aloud.

This new attack promised to be upon Alan's side, and I began to think my share of the fight was at an end, when I heard someone drop softly on the roof.

Then there came a call on the sea pipe, and that was the signal. A knot of them made a rush, cutlass in hand, against the door, and at the same moment the glass of the skylight was dashed in pieces, and a man leaped through and landed on the floor. Before he got his feet, I had clapped a pistol to his back, but at the touch of him, I could no more pull the trigger than I could have flown.

When he felt the pistol, he whipped round and laid hold of me, roaring an oath. At that my courage must have come again, for I shot him in the body. He gave the most horrible groan, and fell to the floor. The foot of a second fellow, whose legs were dangling through the skylight, struck me at the same time upon the head; and at that I snatched another pistol and shot this one through the thigh, so that he slipped through and tumbled in a lump on his companion's body.

I might have stood and stared at them for long, but Alan's shout brought me to my senses. One of the seamen had run in under his guard and caught him about the body. Alan was dirking him with his left hand, but the fellow clung like a leech. Another had his cutlass raised. The door was thronged with faces. I thought we were lost, and catching up my cutlass, fell on them in flank.

But I had not time to be of help. The wrestler dropped at last, and Alan, leaping back to get his distance, ran upon the others like a bull, roaring as he went. They broke before him, turning, running, and falling one against another in their haste. The sword in his hand flashed like quicksilver and at every flash there came the scream of a man hurt. I was still thinking we were lost, when lo! they were all gone, and Alan was driving them along the deck as a sheep dog chases sheep.

He was soon back again, but the seamen continued running, and we heard them tumble one upon another into the forecastle, and clap to the hatch.

The roundhouse was like a shambles. Three were dead inside, another lay in his death agony across the threshold. Alan and I were victorious and unhurt. He embraced me and cried, "David, I love you like a brother. And O, man, am I no a bonny fighter?" Thereupon he tumbled the four enemies out-of-doors one after the other. As he did so, he kept singing to himself, like a man trying to recall an air, only what *he* was trying was to make one. Presently he sat down upon the table, sword in hand. The air all the time began to run a little clearer, and then he burst with a great voice into a Gaelic song. He sang it often afterwards, and the thing became popular, so that I have heard it, and had it explained to me, many's the time. I have translated it here (but not in verse, of which I have no skill):

This is the song of the sword of Alan;
The smith made it,
The fire set it;
Now it shines in the hand of Alan Breck.

Their eyes were many and bright,
Swift were they to behold,
Many the hands they guided;
The sword was alone.

The dun deer troop over the hill,
They are many, the hill is one;
The dun deer vanish,
The hill remains.

Come to me from the hills of heather,
Come from the isles of the sea.
O far-beholding eagles,
Here is your meat.

Now this song which he made in the hour of our victory is something less than just to me. Of the six either killed outright or thoroughly disabled, two fell by my hand. Of the four more who were hurt, one (and he not the least important) got his hurt from me. So, altogether, I did my fair share and might have claimed a place in Alan's verses. But poets have to think upon their rhymes, and in good prose talk, Alan always did me more than justice.

In the meanwhile, what with the scurry and strain of our fighting, I was glad to stagger to a seat. The thought of the two men I had shot sat upon me like a nightmare, and all upon a sudden, before I could guess what was following, I began to sob and cry like any child.

Alan clapped my shoulder, and said I was a brave lad and wanted nothing but sleep. "I'll take the first watch," said he. "You've done well by me, David, first and last."

So I made up my bed on the floor and he took the first spell, pistol in hand and sword on knee, three hours by the captain's watch upon the wall. Then I took my turn of three hours, before the end of which it was broad day, with a smooth, rolling sea and a heavy rain that drummed upon the roof.

All my watch, there was nothing stirring; and by the banging of the helm, I knew they had no one at the tiller. It was a mercy the night was so still, for the wind had gone down as soon as the rain began. Even as it was, the brig must have drifted near the islands of the Hebrides, for at last, looking out of the roundhouse door, I saw the great stone hills of Skye.

CHAPTER VI

The captain knuckles under and I hear of the "Red Fox"

ALAN AND I SAT DOWN to breakfast about six of the clock. The floor was covered with blood and broken glass, which took away my hunger. In all other ways we were in an agreeable situation, having at command all the drink in the ship and all the dainty part of what was eatable. The richest part of it was that the two thirstiest men that ever came out of Scotland (Mr. Shuan being dead) were now shut in the forepart of the ship, condemned to what they hated most—cold water.

"And depend upon it," Alan said, "we shall hear more of them ere long. Ye may keep a man from the fighting, but never from his bottle."

We made good company for each other. Alan, indeed, expressed himself most lovingly, and cut me off one of the silver buttons from his coat. "I had them," says he, "from my father, and now give ye one as a keepsake for last night's work. Wherever ye show it, the friends of Alan Breck will come around you."

He said this as if he commanded armies. Indeed, much as I admired his courage, I was always in danger of smiling at his vanity, and had I not kept my countenance, I would be afraid to think what a quarrel might have followed.

As soon as we were through with our meal, he found a clothes-brush in the captain's locker, and taking off his coat, began to brush away the stains with such care and labor as I supposed to have been only usual with women. To be sure, it belonged to a king, as he said, and so behoved to be royally looked after. Indeed, when I saw him pluck out the threads where the button had been cut away, I put a higher value on his gift.

He was still so engaged when we were hailed by Mr. Riach from the deck, asking for a parley. I, climbing through the skylight and sitting on the edge of it, pistol in hand and with a bold front, though inwardly in fear of broken glass, bade him speak out. He came to the edge of the roundhouse and stood on a coil of rope, so that his chin was on a level with the roof. I do not think he had been very forward in the battle (he had got off with nothing worse than a blow upon the cheek), but he looked out of heart and very weary. "This is a bad job," said he at last, shaking his head. "The captain would like to speak at the window with your friend."

"And how do we know what treachery he means?"

"He means none, David, and if he did, I'll tell ye the truth, we couldnae get the men to follow. More than the men, it's me. I'm frightened, Davie." He smiled across at me. "No, what we want is to be shut of him."

Thereupon I consulted with Alan. The parley was agreed and parole given upon either side. But this was not the whole of Mr. Riach's business. He now begged me for a dram with such reminders of his former kindness that at last I handed him a pannikin of brandy. He carried it down upon the deck, to share it (I suppose) with his superior.

A little after, the captain came to a window and stood in the rain, with his arm in a sling, looking stern and pale, and so old that my heart smote me for having fired upon him. Alan at once held a pistol in his face.

"Put that thing up!" said the captain. "Have I not passed my word, sir? Or do ye seek to affront me?"

"Captain," says Alan, "last night ye arglebargled like an apple-wife, then passed me your word and gave me your hand. Ye ken very well the upshot. Be damned to your word!"

"Well, sir," said Hoseason, "ye'll get little good by swearing. Ye've made a sore hash of my brig. I haven't hands enough left to work her, and there is nothing left me, sir, but to put back into the port of Glasgow. There ye will find them that are better able to talk to you."

"Ay?" said Alan. "And faith, I have a bonny tale for them. Fifteen tarry sailors on one side, and a man and a boy on the other. It's peetiful!" Hoseason flushed red. "No," continued Alan, "that'll no do. Ye'll just have to set me ashore as we agreed."

"But my first officer is dead—ye ken best how," said Hoseason

42

bitterly. "There's none of the rest of us acquaint with this very dangerous coast, sir."

"I give ye your choice," says Alan. "Set me on dry ground in Appin or Ardgour, Morven or Morar; or, in brief, within thirty miles of my own country, but not in a country of the Campbells. That's a broad target. If ye miss that, ye must be as feckless at the sailoring as I have found ye at the fighting."

"All this will cost money, sir," said the captain.

"Well, sir," says Alan, "thirty guineas, if ye land me on the sea-side, and sixty, as we arranged, if ye put me in the Linnhe Loch."

"It's to risk the brig," said Hoseason, "and your lives."

"Take it or want it," says Alan.

"Could ye pilot us at all?" asked Hoseason, frowning.

"It's doubtful," said Alan. "But I have been often enough picked up and set down upon this coast, and should ken something of it."

The captain shook his head, still frowning. "Be it as ye will. As soon as I get a slant of wind I'll put it in hand. But there's one thing more. We may meet with a King's ship and she may lay us aboard with no blame of mine. If that was to befall, sir, ye might leave the money."

"Captain," says Alan, "if ye see a pennant, it shall be your part to run away. And now, as I hear you're a little short of brandy in the forepart, I'll offer you a change: a bottle of brandy against two buckets of water."

This last clause of the treaty was duly executed on both sides, and Alan and I could at last wash out the roundhouse.

Shortly after we had done this, a northeasterly breeze sprang up which blew off the rain and brought out the sun.

At dawn we had lain becalmed between the Isle of Canna and Isle Eriska. To get from there to the Linnhe Loch, the straight course was through the narrows of the Sound of Mull. But the captain had no chart; he was afraid to trust his brig so deep among the islands, and preferred to go by west of Tiree and come up under the southern coast of the Isle of Mull.

The breeze held and the day was very pleasant, sailing, as we were, in a bright sunshine with many mountainous islands upon different sides. Alan and I sat in the roundhouse with the doors open on each side, the wind being straight astern, and smoked a pipe or two of the captain's fine tobacco.

It was at this time we heard each other's stories. I showed the example, telling him all my misfortune, which he heard with great good nature. Only, when I came to mention that good friend of mine, Mr. Campbell the minister, Alan fired up and cried out that he hated all of that name.

"Why, Alan," I cried, "what ails ye at the Campbells?"

"Well," says he, "ye ken that I am an Appin Stewart. The Campbells have long harried those of my name and got lands of us by treachery—but never with the sword." With the last word he cried loudly and brought down his fist upon the table. But I paid the less attention to this, for I knew it was usually said by those who have the underhand.

"There's more than that," he continued; "lying words and papers, tricks fit for a pedlar, to make a man the more angry."

"You that are so wasteful of your buttons," said I, "I can hardly think you would be a good judge of business."

"Ah!" says he, smiling again. "I got my wastefulness from the same man I got the buttons from. My poor father was the prettiest man of his kindred and the best swordsman in the Hielands, Davie, and in all the world, I should ken, for it was him that taught me. But he left me little besides my breeks to cover me. And that was how I came to enlist, which was a black spot upon my character at the best of times, and would still be sore for me if I fell among redcoats."

"What," cried I, "were you in the English army?"

"That was I," said Alan. "But I deserted to the right side at Preston Pans—and that's some comfort."

I could scarcely share this view, holding desertion for an unpardonable fault. But I was wiser than say my thought. "Dear, dear," says I, "the punishment is death."

"Ay," said he. "But I have the King of France's commission in my pocket, which would be some protection."

"I misdoubt it much," said I.

"I have doubts mysel'," said Alan, dryly.

"And, good Heaven, man," cried I, "you that are a condemned rebel, a deserter, and a man of the French King's—what tempts ye back into this country?"

"Tut!" says Alan. "I have been back every year since 'Forty-six. I weary for my friends and country, for the heather and the deer. And while I pick up a few recruits to serve the King of France, I attend to the business of Ardshiel, the captain of my clan. Ye see, David," he said, "he that was all his life so great a man is now brought down to live in a French town like a poor person. I have seen him buying butter in the marketplace. This is not only a pain but a disgrace to us of his clan. There are the bairns forby, the children of Ardshiel, that must be learned their letters and how to hold a sword, in that far country. Now, the tenants of Appin have to pay a rent to King George, but they are true to their chief, and what with love and a bit of pressure, they scrape up a second rent for Ardshiel. Well, David, I'm the hand that carries it." And he struck his belt so that the guineas rang.

"Do they pay both?" cried I.

"Ay, David," said he. "And it's wonderful to me how little pressure is needed. But that's the handiwork of my good kinsman and Ardshiel's half brother, James Stewart of the Glens. He gets the money in, and does the management."

"I'm a Whig, but I call it noble," I cried.

"Ay," said he, "ye're a Whig, but ye're a gentleman; and that's what does it. Now, if ye were one of the cursed race of Campbell, ye would gnash your teeth to hear tell of it. If ye were the Red Fox . . ." At that name he ceased speaking, very grim of face.

"And who is the Red Fox?" I asked, daunted, but still curious.

"Well, I'll tell you that," cried Alan. "When the good cause went down at Culloden and horses rode over the best blood of the north, Ardshiel, his lady, and his bairns had to flee. The English rogues that couldnae come at his life stripped him of his powers and lands; they plucked the weapons from the hands of his clansmen and the very clothes off their backs—so that it's now a sin to wear a tartan plaid or a kilt. One thing they couldnae kill: the love the clansmen bore their chief. These guineas are the proof of it. And now, in there steps a Campbell, redheaded Colin of Glenure—"

"Is that him you call the Red Fox?" said I.

"Will ye bring me his brush?" cried Alan, fiercely. "Ay, that's the man. In he steps, and gets papers from King George, to be so-called King's Factor on the lands of Appin. By and by it came to his ears how the poor farmers and the crofters were wringing their very plaids to get a second rent for Ardshiel; and the black Campbell blood in him ran wild. What! Should a Stewart get a bite of bread, and him not be able to prevent it?" Alan stopped to swallow down his anger. "Well, what does he do? He declares all the farms to let, thinking, 'I'll soon get other tenants that'll overbid these Stewarts, Maccolls, and Macrobs (these are all names in my clan, David), and then Ardshiel will have to hold his bonnet on a French roadside.'"

"Well," said I, "what followed?"

Alan laid down his pipe, which had long since gone out, and set his two hands upon his knees. "Ay, ye'll never guess that! These same Stewarts, that had two rents to pay, offered him a better price than any Campbell."

"Well, Alan," said I, "that is a strange and fine story, and Whig as I may be, I am glad the man was beaten."

"It's little ye ken of the Red Fox. Him beaten?" replied Alan. "No: nor will be, till his blood's on the hillside! But if the day comes that I can find time and leisure for a bit of hunting, there grows not enough heather in all Scotland to hide him from my vengeance!"

"Alan," said I, "ye are neither wise nor Christian to blow off so many words of anger. They will do the Fox no harm, and yourself no good. Tell me plainly, what did he next?"

"Well, David," said Alan, "he aimed to starve Ardshiel. And since them that fed him in his exile wouldnae be bought out—right or wrong, he would drive them out. Therefore he sent for lawyers and redcoats. The folk of that country must all pack and tramp out of the place where they were bred and fed. And who are to succeed them? Bare-leggit beggars! King George is to whistle for his rents and spread his butter thinner: what cares Red Colin? If he can hurt Ardshiel, he has his wish."

"Be sure," said I, "if they take less rents, Government has a finger in the pie. It's not this Campbell's fault—it's his orders. If ye killed him tomorrow there would be another factor in his shoes."

"Ye're a good lad in a fight," said Alan, "but, man, ye have Whig blood in ye!" He spoke kindly enough, but there was so much anger under his contempt that I thought it wise to change the conversation. I expressed my wonder how, with the Highlands covered with troops, a man in his situation could come and go without arrest.

"It's easier than ye would think," said Alan. "A bare hillside is like a road. If there's a sentry at one place, ye go by another. Everywhere there are friends' houses. A soldier covers nae mair of the country than his boot soles. I have sat in a heather bush within six feet of a sentry and learned a real bonny tune from his whistling.

"And then, it's no sae bad now as it was in 'Forty-six," he continued. "The Hielands are what they call pacified. But what I would like to ken, David, is for how long, with men like Ardshiel in exile and men like the Red Fox birling the wine and oppressing the poor at home? It's a thing to decide what folk'll bear, and what they will not. Or why would Red Colin be riding all over my poor country and never a pretty lad to put a bullet in him?"

And with this Alan fell into a muse, and for a long time sat very sad and silent.

CHAPTER VII

The loss of the brig

IT WAS ALREADY LATE AT NIGHT when Hoseason clapped his head into the roundhouse door. "Here," said he, "come out and see if ye can pilot."

"Is this one of your tricks?" asked Alan.

"Do I look like tricks?" cries the captain. "I have other things to think of—my brig's in danger!"

47

By the concerned look of his face and by the sharp tones in which he spoke of his brig, it was plain to both of us he was in deadly earnest, so Alan and I stepped on deck.

The moon, which was nearly full, shone brightly; the sky was clear, the wind now blew hard and was bitter cold. The brig was close hauled, so as to round the southwest corner of the Island of Mull, which lay upon the larboard bow, but she tore through the seas at a great rate, pursued by a westerly swell.

Altogether it was no such ill night to keep the seas in, and I had begun to wonder what it was that sat so heavily upon the captain, when he pointed and cried to us to look. Away on the lee bow, a fountain rose out of the moonlit sea and we heard a low roar. "What do ye call that?" he asked.

"The sea breaking on a reef," said Alan. "Now ye ken where it is, what better would ye have?"

"Ay," said Hoseason, "if it were the only one."

And sure enough as he spoke, there came a second fountain farther to the south.

"There!" said Hoseason. "Ye see for yourself. If I had kent of these reefs, or if Shuan had been spared, not six hundred guineas would have made me risk my brig in sic a stoneyard! But you, sir, that was to pilot us, have ye never a word?"

"I'm thinking," said Alan, "these'll be the Torran Rocks."

Mr. Riach and the captain looked at each other. "There's a way through them, I suppose?" said Hoseason.

"I am nae pilot," said Alan, "but it runs in my mind that it is clearer under the land."

"So?" said Hoseason. "Then we'll have to come as near in about the end of Mull as we can take her, Mr. Riach. Even then we'll have the land to keep the wind off us, and that stoneyard on our lee. Well, we're in for it now." With that he gave an order to the steersman.

As there were only five men on deck, counting the officers (these being all that were both fit and willing for their work), it fell to Mr. Riach to go aloft, and he sat there hailing the deck with news of all he saw. "It does seem clearer by the land," he cried after a while.

"Well, we'll try your way," said Hoseason to Alan. "But I think I might as well trust to a blind fiddler. Pray God you're right."

As we got nearer to the turn of the land the reefs began to be sown here and there on our very path. Mr. Riach cried down to us to change the course; sometimes, none too soon, for one reef was so close that when a sea burst upon it the sprays fell upon the brig's deck and wetted us like rain.

The brightness of the night showed us these perils as clearly as by day, which was the more alarming. It showed me, too, the captain standing as steady as steel by the steersman. I saw both he and Mr. Riach were brave in their own trade, and I admired them all the more because I found Alan very white.

"David," says he, "this is no the kind of death I fancy!"

"What, Alan!" I cried. "You're not afraid?"

"No," said he, wetting his lips, "but you'll allow it's a cold ending."

By this time, still hugging the wind and the land, we had got round Iona and begun to come alongside Mull. The tide at the tail of the land ran very strong, and threw the brig about. Two hands were put to the helm, and Hoseason himself would sometimes lend a help. Then Mr. Riach announced from the top that he saw clear water ahead.

"Ye were right," said Hoseason to Alan. "Ye have saved the brig, sir. I'll mind that when we come to clear accounts." And I believe he not only meant what he said, but would have done it; so high a place did the *Covenant* hold in his affections.

But this is matter only for conjecture, things having gone otherwise than he forecast.

"Keep her away a point," sings out Mr. Riach. "Reef to windward."

And just at the same time the tide caught the brig, and threw the wind out of her sails. She came round into the wind like a top, and the next moment struck the reef with such a dunch as threw us all upon the deck, and came near to shake Mr. Riach from the mast.

I was on my feet in a minute. The reef was close in under the southwest end of Mull, and, as I learned later, off a little isle they call Earraid.

Sometimes the swell broke clean over us; sometimes it only ground the brig upon the reef, so that we could hear her beat herself to pieces; what with the great noise of the sails, the singing of the wind, the flying of the spray, and the sense of danger, I could scarcely understand the things I saw.

I observed Mr. Riach and the seamen busy round the skiff, and ran over to assist them. It was no very easy task, for the skiff lay amidships and the breaking of the seas continually forced us to give over, but we all wrought like horses while we could. Meanwhile such of the wounded as could move came to help, while the rest in their bunks harrowed me with screaming and begging to be saved. It seemed the captain was struck stupid. His brig was like wife and child to him and he stood holding on to the shrouds, talking to himself and groaning whenever she hammered on the rock.

All the time of our working at the boat, I remember only that I asked Alan, looking at the shore, what country it was. He answered, it was the worst possible for him, a land of the Campbells.

Well, we had the boat ready to be launched, when a man sang out pretty shrill: "For God's sake, hold on!" There followed a sea so huge that it lifted and canted the brig right over on her beam. Whether the cry came too late, or my hold was too weak, I know not, but at the sudden tilting of the ship I was cast clean over the bulwarks into the sea.

I went down, and drank my fill, and came up and got a blink of the moon, and then down again. They say a man sinks a third time for good. I cannot be made like other folk, then, for I would not like to write how often I went down or came up again. All the while I was being hurled along in the tide race, beaten upon, choked, and then swallowed whole. The thing was so distracting to my wits that I was neither sorry nor afraid.

Presently, I found I was holding to a spar, and then, all of a sudden, I was in quiet water. I was amazed to see how far I had traveled from the brig. I hailed her, but she was already out of cry. She was still holding together, but whether or not they had launched the boat, I could not see.

I now lay quite becalmed, and began to feel that a man can die of cold as well as of drowning. The shores of Earraid were close in. I could see in the moonlight the sparkling of the mica in the rocks. I had no skill of swimming, but I laid hold upon the spar and kicked out with both feet. Hard work it was, and mortally slow, but in an hour of kicking and splashing, I had got well in between the points of a sandy bay surrounded by low hills.

The moon shone clear, and I thought I had never seen a place so desolate. But it was dry land, and when at last I could leave the spar and wade ashore, I was grateful to God as I trust I have been often, though never with more cause.

CHAPTER VIII

The islet

IT WAS HALF PAST TWELVE, and though the wind was broken by the land, it was a cold night. I took off my shoes and walked to and fro upon the sand, beating my breast with infinite weariness. There was no sound of man or cattle; only the surf broke in the distance, which put me in mind of my perils and those of my friend.

As day began to break I put on my shoes and climbed a hill— the ruggedest scramble I ever undertook. When I got to the top, there was no sign of the brig, which must have sunk. The boat, too, was nowhere to be seen. There was never a sail upon the ocean, and no house in what I could see of the land.

I was afraid to think what had befallen my shipmates, and afraid to look longer at so empty a scene. So, with my belly now beginning to ache with hunger, I set off eastward along the south coast, hoping to find a house where I might warm myself, and perhaps get news of those I had lost. At the worst, the sun would soon rise and dry my clothes.

After a little, my way was stopped by an inlet of the sea, which seemed to run deep into the land. As I had no means to get across, I must needs change my direction to go about the end of it. It was the roughest kind of walking, for the whole, not only of Earraid, but of the neighboring part of Mull (which they call the Ross), is nothing but a jumble of granite rocks with heather in among. At first the creek kept narrowing, but presently, to my surprise, it began to widen out again. I had no notion of the truth until I came to rising ground, and it burst upon me that I was cast upon a little barren isle, and cut off on every side by the salt seas.

Instead of the sun rising to dry me, it came on to rain with a thick mist. I shivered and wondered what to do. All at once, the spar came in my head. What had carried me through the tide race would surely serve me to cross this little quiet creek in safety. I set off, across the top of the isle to fetch it. It was a weary tramp, and whether with the sea salt or because I was growing fevered, I was distressed with thirst, and had to stop to drink the peaty water out of the small ravines.

I came to the bay at last, and at first glance, I thought the spar was farther out than when I left it. The firm sand shelved gradually down, so that I could wade out till the water was almost to my neck. But at that depth my feet began to leave me, and I durst venture no farther. As for the spar, I saw it bobbing very quietly some twenty feet beyond.

At this last disappointment I came ashore, and flung myself down upon the sands and wept.

The time I spent upon the island is still so horrible a thought to me that I must pass it lightly over. In all the books I have read of people cast away, they had either their pockets full of tools, or a chest of things thrown upon the beach with them. I had nothing but money and Alan's silver button and, being inland-bred, I was as much short of knowledge as of means.

I knew that shellfish were counted good to eat, and among the rocks I found periwinkles and limpets, which at first I could scarcely strike from their places, not knowing quickness to be needful. Of these two I made my diet, devouring them raw. At first they seemed delicious. Yet perhaps they were out of season, for I never knew what to expect when I had eaten them, and sometimes I was thrown into a miserable sickness.

All the first day it streamed rain. The island ran like a sop. There was no dry spot to be found, and when I lay down that night, between two boulders that made a kind of roof, my feet were in a bog.

The second day I crossed the island to all sides. It was all desolate and rocky, nothing living on it but game birds which I lacked the means to kill, and the gulls which haunted the outlying rocks. The creek, or strait, that cut off the isle from the mainland of the Ross, opened out on the north into a bay, and the bay again opened into the Sound of Iona. But from a little up the hillside over the bay, I could catch a sight of the houses and the great, ancient church in Iona. I watched the smoke go up from those homesteads, and when I was wet and cold, and had my head half turned with loneliness, this sight kept hope alive. It seemed impossible that I should be left to die within view of a church tower and men's houses. But the second day passed and no help came.

The next morning I saw a red deer standing in the rain on the top of the island, but he had scarce seen me before he trotted off upon the other side. I supposed he must have swum across the strait, though what should bring any creature to Earraid was more than I could fancy.

A little after, as I was jumping about after limpets, a guinea piece fell upon a rock in front of me and glanced off into the sea. When the sailors gave me my money back, they kept my father's leather purse, so that I had been carrying my gold loose in a pocket with the button. I now saw there must be a hole, and clapped my hand to the place in a great hurry. But this was to lock the stable door after the steed was stolen. I had left the shore at Queensferry with near fifty pounds; now I found no more than three guinea pieces and the silver button.

My plight was truly pitiful. My clothes were beginning to rot; my stockings in particular were quite worn through; my throat was very sore, and my strength had much abated. And the worst was not yet come.

In the afternoon, the sun came out and I lay down on the top of a high rock on the northwest of Earraid to dry myself. The comfort of the sunshine set me thinking hopefully of my deliverance and I scanned the sea with fresh interest.

All of a sudden, a coble with a brown sail and a pair of fishers aboard came flying round a corner of the isle. I shouted out, and then fell on my knees on the rock and reached up my hands and prayed to them. There was no doubt they observed me, for they cried out in the Gaelic tongue, and laughed. But the boat flew on, right before my eyes, for Iona.

I could not believe such wickedness, and ran along the shore from rock to rock, crying on them piteously. Even after they were out of reach of my voice, I still cried and waved to them. When they were quite gone, I wept and roared like a wicked child, tearing up the turf with my nails, and grinding my face in the earth. When I was a little over my anger, I ate again, but with such loathing of the mess as I could now scarce control. Sure enough, the fishes poisoned me again. I had a fit of shuddering which clucked my teeth together, and there came on me a dreadful sense of illness. I thought I should have died, and made my peace with God, forgiving all men, even my uncle and the fishers. As soon as I had thus made up my mind to the worst, clearness came upon me: I observed the night was falling dry; my clothes were dried a good deal; and I got to sleep with even a thought of gratitude.

The next day I found my strength run very low. But the sun shone, the air was sweet, and I was scarce back on my rock before I observed a boat coming down the Sound towards me.

I began at once to hope, but I thought that another disappointment, such as yesterday's, would be more than I could bear. I turned my back, accordingly, upon the sea, and did not look again till I had counted many hundreds. The boat was still heading for the island. I could no longer hold myself back, but ran to the seaside, and out from one rock to another, as far as I could go. My mouth was so dry I must wet it with the seawater before I was able to shout.

And now I was able to perceive it was the same boat and the

same two men as yesterday. But now there was a third man along with them. As soon as they were come within easy speech, they let down their sail and lay quiet. In spite of my supplications, they drew no nearer in, and what frightened me most, the new man tee-heed with laughter as he looked at me.

Then he stood up in the boat and addressed me a long while, speaking fast and with many wavings of his hand. I told him I had no Gaelic. At this he became very angry, and I began to suspect he thought he was talking English. Listening very close, I caught the word "whateffer" several times; but all the rest might have been Greek and Hebrew for me.

"Whatever," said I, to show him I had caught a word.

"Yes, yes," says he, and then he looked at the other men, as much as to say, "I told you I spoke English," and began again as hard as ever in the Gaelic.

This time, with a flash of hope, I picked out another word, "tide." I saw he was always waving his hand towards the mainland of the Ross. "Do you mean when the tide is out?" I cried.

"Yes, yes," said he. "Tide."

At that I turned tail upon their boat (where my adviser had once more begun to tee-hee with laughter), and set off running across the isle as I had never run before. I came out upon the shores of the strait. Sure enough, it was shrunk into a little trickle through which I dashed, the water not above my knees, and landed with a shout on the mainland.

A sea-bred boy would not have stayed a day on Earraid, which is a tidal islet and can be entered and left twice in every twenty-four hours by wading; it was no wonder the fishers had not understood me. The wonder was rather that they had ever guessed my pitiful illusion, and taken the trouble to come back. But for them, I might have left my bones on that island in pure folly. As it was, I paid for it dear, not only in past sufferings, but in my present case; being clothed like a beggarman, scarce able to walk, and in great pain of my sore throat.

I have seen a great many wicked men and fools, and I believe they both get paid in the end; but the fools first.

CHAPTER IX

The lad with the silver button:
through the Isle of Mull and across Morven

THE ROSS OF MULL WAS RUGGED and trackless, like the isle I had just left. I aimed for some smoke I could see and, with great weariness, came upon a house in a little hollow about five at night. It was low and longish, roofed with turf and built of unmortared stones, and on a mound in front of it, an old gentleman sat smoking his pipe in the sun.

With what little English he had, he gave me to understand that my shipmates had got safe ashore, and had broken bread in that very house on the day after.

"Was there one," I asked, "dressed like a gentleman?"

To be sure, he said, the first of them, the one that came alone, wore breeches and stockings, while the rest had sailors' trousers. Then he clapped his hand to his brow, and cried out that I must be the lad with the silver button.

"Why, yes!" said I, in some wonder.

"Well, then," said he, "you are to follow your friend to his country, by Torosay."

The old gentleman (I call him so because of his manners, for his clothes were dropping off his back) then asked me how I had fared. When I had told him my tale, he took me by the hand, led me into his hut (it was no better) and presented me before his wife, as if she had been the Queen and I a duke. The good woman set oatbread before me and a cold grouse, patting my shoulder and smiling to me all the time, for she had no English. The old gentleman brewed me a strong punch which, after I had eaten, threw me in a deep slumber.

The good people let me lie and it was near noon of the next day before I took the road, my throat easier and my spirits restored by good fare and good news. The old gentleman would take no money, and gave me an old bonnet for my head; though I'm free to own I was no sooner out of view of the house, than I washed this gift in a wayside fountain.

Thought I to myself, If these are the wild Highlanders, I only wish my own folk wilder.

I not only started late, but I must have wandered nearly half the time. True, I met plenty of people, grubbing in little miserable fields that would not keep a cat. The Highland dress being forbidden by law since the rebellion (in hopes to break up the clan spirit), some wore only a coat, and carried their trousers on their backs like a useless burthen; others still wore the Highland kilt, but by putting a few stitches between the legs, transformed it into a pair of trousers like a Dutchman's. Few had any English, and these (unless they were beggars who stood on their dignity, and by their account asked alms only to buy snuff) were not very anxious to place it at my service. I knew Torosay to be my destination, and repeated the name to them and pointed; but instead of simply pointing in reply, they would give me a screed of Gaelic that set me foolish.

At last, about eight at night, I came to a lone house, where I was refused admittance until I held up one of my guineas. Thereupon, the man of the house, who had hitherto pretended to have no English, suddenly began to speak as clearly as was needful, and agreed for five shillings to give me a night's lodging and guide me next day to Torosay.

The next morning, we had to go five miles to the house of what he called a rich man to have one of my guineas changed. This was perhaps a rich man for Mull but he would have scarce been thought so in the south, for it took all he had to scrape together twenty shillings in silver. The odd shilling he kept for himself, protesting that he could ill afford to have so great a sum as a guinea lying "locked up." For all that he was very courteous. He made us sit down with his family to dinner, and brewed punch in a fine china bowl, over which my rascal guide grew so merry that he refused to start. So there was nothing for it but to sit and hear Jacobite toasts and Gaelic songs, till all were tipsy and staggering off to bed.

Next day (the fourth of my travels) we were up before five upon the clock, but no sooner had we got out of sight of the house than he told me Torosay lay right in front, and that hilltop (which he pointed out) was my best landmark.

"I care little for that," said I, "since you are going with me."

The cheat answered that he had no English.

"My fine fellow," I said, "I know very well your English comes and goes. Tell me what will bring it back."

"Five shillings mair," said he, "and I will bring ye there."

I offered him two, which he accepted greedily. They carried him not quite two miles; at the end of which, he sat down and took off his brogues like a man about to rest.

"Ha!" said I, now red-hot. "Have you no more English?"

He said impudently, "No."

At that I lifted my hand to strike him and he, drawing a knife from his rags, squatted back and grinned at me like a wildcat. Forgetting everything but my anger, I ran in upon him, put aside his knife with my left, and struck him in the mouth with the right. He was but a little man and he went down before me heavily. His knife flew out of his hand as he fell.

I picked up both that and his brogues, wished him a good morning, and set off upon my way, being sure I had done with that rogue.

In about half an hour, I overtook a great, ragged man, moving fast but feeling before him with a staff. He was quite blind, and told me he was a catechist, which should have put me at my ease. But his face seemed dark and dangerous, and as we began to go on alongside, I saw the butt of a pistol sticking from under the flap of his coat pocket. To carry such a thing was a law offense, and I could not see what a blind religious teacher could be doing with a pistol. But my vanity got the heels of my prudence, and I told him what I had done about my guide.

At the mention of the five shillings he cried out loud.

"Was it too much?" I asked, faltering.

"Too much!" cried he. "Why, I will guide you to Torosay myself for a dram of brandy. And give you the pleasure of my company in the bargain."

I said I did not see how a blind man could be a guide. At that he laughed aloud, and said his stick was eyes enough for an eagle. "See, now," he said, "down there a burn is running. At the head of it stands a small hill with a stone cocked on the top. That's the way to Torosay."

I had to own my wonder.

"Ha," says he with a leer, "that's nothing. Before the Act came out and there were weepons in this country, I could shoot. If ye have a pistol here, I would show ye how it's done."

I said nothing and gave him a wider berth. I could still see the pistol sticking out of his pocket, the sun twinkling on the steel butt.

He then began to question me cunningly, whether I was rich, whether I could change a five-shilling piece for him, and all the time he kept edging up to me and I avoiding him. We were now upon a cattle track crossing the hill towards Torosay and we kept changing sides like dancers in a reel. I took a pleasure in this game of blindman's buff, but the catechist grew angrier and angrier and began to strike for my legs with his staff.

Then I told him that, sure enough, I had a pistol in my pocket as well as he, and if he did not strike due south I would blow his brains out. He at once took himself off, cursing me in Gaelic. I watched him striding along, through bog and brier, tapping with his stick, until he turned the end of the hill and disappeared in the next hollow. Then I struck on again, much better pleased to travel alone than with the two of whom I had just rid myself, one after the other.

At Torosay, looking over to the mainland of Morven, there was an inn where I sat and drank punch with the landlord (or to be more correct, sat up and watched him drink it). I tried him with a sight of Alan's button, but it was plain he had never seen or heard of it.

When I told him of my catechist, he shook his head, and said I was lucky to have got off. "That is Duncan Mackiegh, a very dangerous man," he said. "He can shoot by ear at several yards, and has been often accused of highway robberies, and once of murder. He is always on the road, going from one place to another to hear young folk say their religion. Doubtless, that is a great temptation to the poor man."

At last, when my landlord could drink no more, he showed me to a bed, and I lay down in very good spirits, and in far better health at the end of my long tramp through Mull than I had been at the beginning.

The next morning I found that the skipper of the ferryboat from Torosay to Kinlochaline on the mainland was called Neil Roy Macrob. Since Macrob was one of the names of Alan's clansmen, and Alan himself had sent me to that ferry, I was eager to come to private speech of Neil Roy.

In the crowded boat next morning this was impossible, but once we had put the boat alongside at Kinlochaline, I got him upon one side. "I am seeking Alan Breck Stewart," said I, "and it comes in my mind that you will have news of him." And very foolishly, instead of showing him the button, I sought to pass a shilling in his hand.

At this he drew back. "I am very much affronted," he said, "and this is not the way that one shentleman should behave to another at all. The man you ask for is in France, but if he was in my sporran and your belly full of shillings, I would not hurt a hair upon his body."

I saw I had gone the wrong way to work, and without wasting time upon apologies, showed him the button.

"Aweel," said Neil, "I think ye might have begun with that end of the stick! But if ye are the lad with the silver button, I have the word to see that ye come safe. But if ye will pardon me, never take the name of Alan Breck into your mouth, and never offer your dirty money to a Hieland shentleman."

It was not easy to apologize. I could scarce tell him that I had never dreamed he would set up to be a gentleman. Neil on his part had no wish to prolong his dealings with me, only to fulfill his orders, and he made haste to give me my route. This was to cross Morven, to be set across one loch at Corran and another at Balachulish, and then ask my way to the house of James of the Glens, at Aucharn in Duror of Appin.

MR. BALFOUR OF THE HOUSE OF SHAWS

THE SIEGE OF THE ROUNDHOUSE

THE WRECK OF THE "COVENANT"

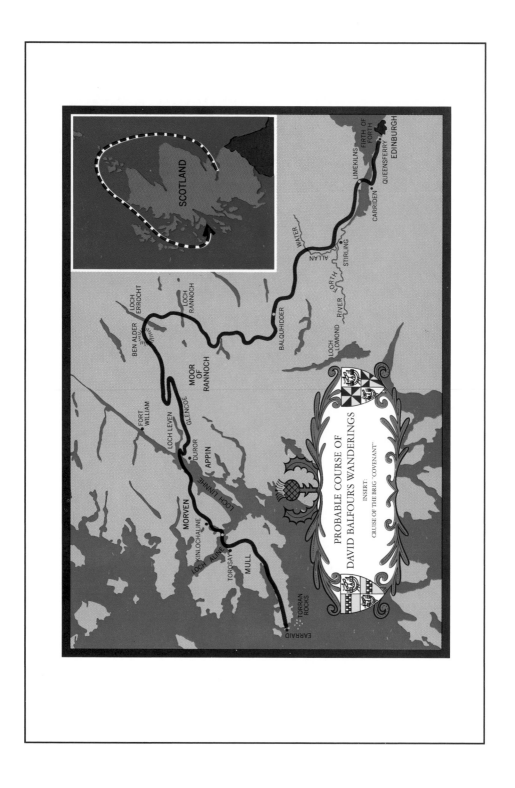

THE MURDERER OF ROY CAMPBELL OF GLENURE

THE TORRENT IN THE VALLEY OF GLENCOE

AT THE CARDS IN CLUNY'S CAGE

THE PARTING

Early in my continued journey I overtook a little, stout, solemn man, reading a book and walking very slowly with his toes turned out, and dressed plainly in a clerical style. He was another catechist, one of those sent out from Edinburgh to evangelize the more savage Highlands, and his name was Henderland. He spoke with the broad south-country tongue, which I was beginning to weary for the sound of; and besides common countryship, we soon found we had a more particular bond of interest. Indeed, when we met, the pious book he was reading was one which my good friend, the minister of Essendean, had translated into Gaelic.

As we walked, he spoke with all the wayfarers we met, and though I could not tell what they discoursed about, I judged he must be well liked in the countryside, for I observed many of them to share a pinch of their snuff with him.

I told him as far in my affairs as I judged wise (as far, that is, as they were none of Alan's), and gave Balachulish as the place I was traveling to, to meet a friend. On his part, he told me much of his work, of hiding priests and Jacobites and many other curiosities of the time and place. He blamed Parliament in several points and this moderation put it in my mind to question him of the Red Fox and the Appin tenants; questions which, I thought, would seem natural enough in the mouth of one traveling to that country.

He said it was a bad business. "It's wonderful," said he, "where the tenants find the money. (Ye don't carry such a thing as snuff, do ye, Mr. Balfour? No. Well, I'm better wanting it.) But doubtless James of the Glens drives these tenants hard. And then there's one they call Alan Breck—"

"Ah!" cried I. "What of him?"

"He's here today and gone tomorrow: a fair heather cat," said Henderland. "He might be glowering at us out of yon bush, and I wouldnae wonder! Ye'll no carry such a thing as snuff, will ye?"

I told him no, and that he had asked the same thing more than once.

"It's highly possible," said he, sighing. "But it seems strange ye shouldnae carry it. However, as I was saying, Alan Breck is a bold customer, well kent to be James's right hand. He would boggle at naething. Maybe if a tenant was to hang back, he would get a dirk in his belly."

"You make a poor story of it, Mr. Henderland," said I. "If it is fear upon both sides, I care to hear no more."

"Na, but there's love too, and self-denial that should put the like of you and me to shame. Even Alan Breck, by all that I hear, is to be respected— Ye'll perhaps think I've been too long in the Hielands?" he added, smiling to me.

I told him not at all, that I had seen much to admire among the Highlanders, and if he came to that, Mr. Campbell himself was a Highlander.

"Ay," said Mr. Henderland, "that's true. It's fine blood."

"And what is Colin Campbell, the King's agent, about?" I asked. "I hear he is to turn the tenants out by force."

"Yes," says he, "but the business has gone back and forth. First, James of the Glens rode to Edinburgh, got some lawyer (a Stewart, nae doubt) and had the proceedings stayed. Then Colin Campbell cam' in again, and now they tell me the first tenants are to flit tomorrow. It's to begin at Duror under James's very windows, which doesnae seem wise by my humble way of it."

"Do you think they'll fight?" I asked.

"Well," says Henderland, "Colin Campbell has the sogers coming. But for all that, if I was his lady wife, I wouldnae be pleased till I got him home again. They're queer customers, the Appin Stewarts; when he's done with them, he has to begin again with their neighbors, the Camerons. There's still a good deal of cold iron lying by in quiet places."

So we continued talking and walking until at last Mr. Henderland proposed that I should lie the night in his house a little beyond Kingairloch. We came to it in the late afternoon, a small house standing alone by the shore of the Linnhe Loch, with the mountains of Appin shining in the sun on the farther side.

We had no sooner come to the door than Mr. Henderland burst rudely past me into the room, caught up a jar and a small spoon, and began ladling snuff into his nose. Then he had a hearty fit of sneezing, and looked round upon me with a rather silly smile.

"It's a vow," says he. "I took a vow upon me that I wouldnae carry it. Doubtless it's a great privation but, when I think upon the martyrs, I think shame to mind it."

As soon as we had eaten (and porridge and whey was the best of the good man's diet) he took a grave face and said he had a duty to perform by Mr. Campbell, and that was to inquire into my state of mind towards God. I was inclined to smile at him since the business of the snuff, but he had not spoken long before he brought the tears into my eyes. And though I was a good deal puffed up with my adventures, I was soon both proud and glad to be on my knees beside the simple old man.

Before we went to bed he offered me sixpence to help me on my way, out of a scanty store he kept in the turf wall of his house. At which excess of goodness I knew not what to do. But he was so earnest with me, that I thought it more mannerly to let him have his way, and so left him poorer than myself.

CHAPTER X

The death of the "Red Fox"

THE NEXT NOON, Mr. Henderland found a man of his flock who was going in his boat across the Linnhe Loch into Appin, and prevailed on him to take me, and thus save me a long day's journey and the price of two public ferries. The water was very deep and still; it was a dark day with clouds, and the sun shining upon little patches. The high mountains on either side were very black and gloomy, but all silver-laced with little watercourses. It seemed a hard country, this of Appin, for people to care about as much as Alan did.

A little after we had started, the sun shone upon a moving clump of scarlet along the waterside to the north. Then came little sparks and lightnings, as though the sun had struck upon bright steel. My boatman supposed it was King George's troops coming from Fort William against the tenants of Appin. Well, it was a sad sight to me; and whether because of my thoughts of Alan, or from something prophetic in my bosom, I had no good will to them.

At last we came so near the point of land at the entering in of Loch Leven that I begged to be set on shore there under the wood of Lettermore in Appin.

This was a wood of birches, growing on a steep, craggy side of a mountain that overhung the loch. A bridle track ran north and south through the midst of it, by the edge of which there was a spring. Here I sat down to eat some oatbread of Mr. Henderland's. I was troubled by what I ought to do, whether I should join an outlaw like Alan, or whether I should act more like a man of sense to tramp back to the south country direct, by my own guidance.

Presently a sound of men and horses came to me through the wood, and at a turning of the path, four travelers came into view. The way was so rough and narrow that they came single and led their horses by the reins. The first was a great, redheaded gentleman, of an imperious and flushed face, who fanned himself with his hat, for he was in a breathing heat. The second, by his black garb and white wig, I took to be a lawyer. The third was a servant, and wore tartan clothes, which showed that his master was of a Highland family, and either an outlaw or else in singular good odor with the Government, since the wearing of tartan was against the Act. If I had been better versed in these things, I would have known the tartan to be of Campbell colors. This servant had a good-sized portmanteau strapped on his horse, and a net of lemons (to brew punch with) hanging at the saddlebow, as was the custom with luxurious travelers in that part. As for the fourth, I knew him at once to be a sheriff's officer.

I had no sooner seen these people than I made up my mind (for no reason that I can tell) to go through with my adventure. I rose up from the bracken and asked the first man the way to Aucharn.

He stopped and looked at me. Then, turning to the lawyer, "Mungo," said he, "there's many a man would think this a warning. Here am I on my road to Duror on the job ye ken, and here, a young lad inquires the way to Aucharn. What seek ye there, lad?"

"The man that lives there," said I.

"James of the Glens," says he musingly, and then to the lawyer: "Is he gathering his people, think ye?"

"Glenure," says the lawyer (and I knew then that I had stopped Colin Roy Campbell of Glenure, him they called the "Red Fox"), "we shall do better to bide where we are, and let the soldiers rally us."

"If you are concerned for me," said I, "I am neither of his people nor yours, but an honest subject of King George."

"Why, well said," replies Glenure. "Your tongue is bold, but I am no unfriend to plainness. I have power here. I am King's Factor and have twelve files of soldiers at my back. If ye had asked me the way to the door of James Stewart on any other day but this, I would have set ye right and bidden ye Godspeed. But today—eh, Mungo?" But just as he turned to look at the lawyer, there came the shot of a firelock from higher up the hill, and Glenure fell upon the road.

"O, I am dead!" he cried, several times over. The lawyer had caught him and held him in his arms, the servant standing over and clasping his hands. Now the wounded man looked from one to another with scared eyes, and there was a change in his voice that went to the heart. "Take care of yourselves," says he. "I am dead."

He tried to open his clothes as if to look for the wound, but his fingers slipped on the buttons. With that he gave a great sigh, his head rolled on his shoulder, and he passed away.

The lawyer said never a word, but his face was as sharp as a pen and as white as the dead man's. The servant broke out crying and weeping, like a child, and I stood staring at them in horror. The sheriff's officer had run back to hasten the coming of the soldiers.

At last the lawyer laid down the dead man upon the road, and his movement brought me to my senses. I began to scramble up the hill, crying out, "The murderer! The murderer!"

So little time had elapsed, that when I got to the top of the first steepness and could see some of the open mountain, the murderer was still moving away at no great distance. He was a big man, in a black coat, and carried a long fowling piece.

"Here!" I cried. "I see him!"

At that the murderer gave a quick look over his shoulder and began to run. The next moment he was lost in a fringe of birches. He came out again on the steep upper side, where I could see him climbing like a jackanapes. Then he dipped behind a shoulder and I saw him no more.

I was now at the edge of the upper wood. The lawyer and the sheriff's officer were standing just above the road, crying and waving to me to come back. On their left, the redcoats, musket in hand, were beginning to struggle out of the lower wood.

"Why should I come back?" I cried. "Come you on!"

"Ten pounds if ye take that lad!" cried the lawyer. "He's an accomplice. He was posted here to hold us in talk."

At those words my heart came in my mouth with quite a new kind of terror. It is one thing to stand the danger of your life, and quite another to run the peril of both life and character. The soldiers began to spread, some of them to move towards me, and still I stood amazed and helpless.

"Duck in here among the trees," said a voice close by.

Indeed, I scarce knew what I was doing, but I obeyed. As I did so, I heard the firelocks bang and the balls whistle in the birches. Just inside the shelter of the trees I found Alan Breck standing, with a fishing rod. He gave me no salutation; only "Come!" says he, and set off running along the mountainside towards Balachulish, and I, like a sheep, followed him.

Now we ran among the birches; now stooped behind low humps upon the mountainside; now crawled on all fours among the heather. My heart seemed bursting against my ribs. I had neither time to think nor breath to speak with. Only I wondered at seeing Alan, every now and then, straighten himself to his full height and look back—and every time he did so, there came a great faraway cheering and crying of the soldiers.

Quarter of an hour later, Alan clapped down flat in the heather and turned to me. "Now," said he, "it's earnest. Do as I do, for your life."

And at the same speed, but now with infinitely more precaution, we traced back again across the mountainside. At last Alan threw himself down in the upper wood of Lettermore, where I had found him at the first, and lay, with his face in the bracken, panting like a dog.

My own sides so ached and my head so swam that I lay beside him like one dead.

CHAPTER XI

I flee with Alan to the House of Fear

ALAN WAS THE FIRST to come round. He rose, went to the border of the wood, peered out a little, and then returned and sat down.

"Well," said he, "yon was a hot burst, David."

I said nothing, nor so much as lifted my face. I had seen murder done, a great ruddy, jovial gentleman struck out of life in a moment. The pity of that sight was but a part of my concern. Here was murder done upon the man Alan hated; here was Alan skulking in the trees and running from the troops; and whether his was the hand that fired or only the head that ordered, signified but little. By my way of it, my only friend in that wild country was blood-guilty in the first degree and I held him in horror.

"Are ye still wearied?" he asked again.

"No," said I, still with my face in the bracken. "I can speak now. You and me must part. I liked you well, Alan, but your ways are not mine, and they're not God's."

"I will hardly part from ye, David, without some reason," said he gravely.

"Alan," said I, "what is the sense of this? Ye ken very well yon Campbellman lies in his blood upon the road."

He was silent awhile. Then says he, "Did ever ye hear the story of the Man of the Good People?"—by which he meant the fairies.

"No," said I, "nor do I want to hear it."

"With your permission, Mr. Balfour, I will tell it you, whatever. The man, ye should ken, was cast upon a rock in the sea, where the Good People used to rest as they went to Ireland. The man cried so sore, if he could just see his little bairn before he died, that at last the king of the Good People took peety upon him, and had the bairn brought back in a bag and laid it down beside the man where he lay sleeping. So when the man woke, there was something in a bag beside him that moved. Well, it seems he was one of these gentry that think the worst of things; for security, he stuck his dirk through that bag before he opened it, and there was his bairn dead. I am thinking, Mr. Balfour, that you and the man are very much alike."

"Do you mean you had no hand in it?" cried I, sitting up.

"I will tell you first of all, Mr. Balfour of Shaws, as one friend to another," said Alan, "that if I were going to kill a gentleman, it would not be in my own country, to bring trouble on my clan; and I would not go wanting sword and gun, and with a long fishing rod upon my back."

"Well," said I, "that's true!"

"And now," continued Alan, taking out his dirk and laying his hand upon it, "I swear upon the Holy Iron I had neither part nor thought in it."

"I thank God for that!" cried I, and offered my hand.

He did not appear to see it. "And here is a great deal of work about a Campbell!" said he. "They are not so scarce, that I ken!"

"At least," said I, "you cannot justly blame me, for you know very well what you told me in the brig. But I thank God again the temptation and the act are different." And I could say no more for the moment. "Do you know that man in the black coat who did it?" I added.

"I have nae clear mind about his coat," said Alan, cunningly, "but it sticks in my head that it was blue. He gaed very close by me to be sure, but it's a strange thing that I should just have been tying my brogues. I've a grand memory for forgetting, David."

"One thing I saw clearly," said I, half angered, half in a mind to laugh at his evasions, "and that was that you exposed yourself and me to draw the soldiers."

"It's very likely," said Alan; "and so would any gentleman.

Them that havenae dipped their hands in any little difficulty should be mindful of them that have. That is good Christianity."

Alan looked so innocent, and was in such clear good faith in what he said, that I gave up. His morals were all tail-first but he was ready to give his life for them, such as they were. "Alan," said I, "I'll not say it's good Christianity as I understand it, but it's good enough. And here I offer ye my hand for the second time."

Whereupon he gave me both of his, saying surely he could forgive me anything. Then he said we had not much time; the whole of Appin would now be searched and everyone obliged to give a good account of himself, and that we must both flee that country: he, because he was a deserter, and I, because I was certainly involved in the murder.

"I have no fear of the justice of my country," says I.

"As if this was your country!" said he. "This is a Campbell that's been killed. It'll be tried in Inverara, the Campbells' head place, with fifteen Campbells in the jury box and the biggest Campbell of all, the Duke of Argyle, on the bench. Justice, David? The Duke's a Whig, nae doubt, but I would never deny he was a good chieftain to his clan. What would the Campbell clan think if there was a Campbell shot, and naebody hanged, and their own chief the Justice General? I have often observed that you Low-country bodies have no clear idea of what's right and wrong."

At this I did laugh out loud, when to my surprise Alan laughed as merrily as myself. "Na, na," said he, "we're in the Hielands, David. When I tell ye to run, take my word and run."

I asked him whither we should flee. As he told me "to the Lowlands," I was better inclined to go with him, for I was growing impatient to get back and have the upper hand of my uncle.

"I'll chance it, Alan," said I. "I'll go with you."

"But mind you," said Alan, "it's no small thing. Your bed shall be the moorcock's, your life shall be like the hunted deer's, and ye shall sleep with your hand upon your weapons. But ye havenae other chance. Either take to the heather with me, or hang."

"And that's a choice easily made," said I; and we shook hands.

"Now let's take another keek at the redcoats," says Alan, and he led me to the northeastern fringe of the wood. We could see a great side of mountain, running down steep into the loch, and away towards Balachulish, little red soldiers dipping up and down over hill and howe and growing smaller every minute. "Ay," said Alan, smiling, "they'll be gey weary before they've got to the end of that employ! And so you and me, David, can strike for Aucharn, where I must get my French clothes and arms and money to carry us along. Then, David, we'll cry, 'Forth, Fortune!' and take a cast among the heather."

On the way to Aucharn, Alan narrated his adventures. It appears that after the huge wave had passed, he had one last glimpse of me clinging to the spar. It was this that put him in hope I would get to land, and made him leave those messages which had brought me to Appin.

Meanwhile, those still on the brig had got the skiff launched, when a second wave, greater than the first, heaved the brig out of her place. Her stern was thrown in the air, and the bows plunged under the sea. There were still two men lying impotent in their bunks, and these began to call out aloud, with such harrowing cries that all on deck tumbled into the skiff and fell to their oars. They were not two hundred yards away when a third great wave lifted the brig clean over the reef, and the sea closed over the *Covenant* of Dysart.

They pulled ashore, and had scarce set foot upon the beach when Hoseason bade them lay hands upon Alan, crying that here was both revenge and wealth upon a single cast. It was seven against one and the sailors began to spread out and come behind him.

"And then," said Alan, "that little man Riach took up the clubs for me, and asked the men if they werenae feared of a judgment, and says, 'Dod, I'll put my back to the Hielandman's mysel'.' He cried to me to run, and indeed, I ran. The last that I saw, they were all in a knot upon the beach not agreeing very well together. But I thought it would be better no to wait. Ye see, there's a strip of Campbells in that end of Mull, which is no good company for a gentleman like me. If it hadnae been for that I would have waited and looked for ye mysel', let alone giving a hand to the little man."

The clouds settled in as we were walking, so that the night fell, for that season, extremely dark, and I could by no means see how Alan directed himself over the rough mountainsides.

At last, we came to the top of a brae and saw lights below us. A house door stood open and let out a beam of fire and candle-light. Round the house five or six persons hurried about, each carrying a lighted brand.

"James must have tint his wits," said Alan. "If this was the soldiers instead of you and me, he would be in a bonny mess. But I daresay he'll have a sentry on the road, and he would ken no soldier would find the way we came."

Hereupon he whistled three times, in a particular manner. At the first sound of it, the moving torches came to a stand, as if the bearers were affrighted, but at the third, the bustle began again as before. Having thus set folks' minds at rest, we came down the brae, and were met at a yard gate (the place was a well-doing farm) by a tall, handsome man of more than fifty, who cried out to Alan in the Gaelic.

"James Stewart," said Alan, "I will ask ye to speak in Scotch, for here is a young laird with me that has nane of the other. This is him," he added, putting his arm through mine, "but I am thinking it will be the better for his health if we give his name the go-by."

James of the Glens greeted me courteously enough. Then he turned to Alan. "This has been a dreadful accident," he cried, and wrung his hands. "It will bring trouble on the country."

"Hoots!" said Alan. "Ye must take the sour with the sweet, man. Colin Roy is dead. Be thankful!"

"By my troth," said James, "I wish he was alive again! It's all very fine to blow and boast beforehand. But now it's done, who's to bear the blame? The accident fell in Appin—it's Appin that must pay, and I am a man that has a family."

I looked about me. Servants were digging in the thatch of the farm buildings and bringing out weapons of war; others carried them away, and by the sound of mattock blows further down the brae, I suppose they buried them. There prevailed no kind of order in their efforts. Men struggled for the same gun and ran into each other with their burning torches. They seemed overborne with panic and their speech sounded both anxious and angry.

It was about this time that a lassie came out of the house carrying a pack or bundle. "What's that she has?" Alan asked.

"We're just setting the house in order," said James, in his frightened and somewhat fawning way. "They'll search Appin with candles, and we must have things straight. These will be your French clothes. We'll bury them, I believe."

"Bury my French clothes!" cried Alan. "Troth, no!" And he laid hold upon the packet and retired into the barn to shift himself.

James took me into the kitchen, and sat down with me at table, frowning and biting his fingers. From time to time, he gave me a word or two and a poor smile, and then went back into his private terrors. His wife sat by the fire and wept, with her face in her hands. His eldest son was crouched upon the floor, running over a great mass of papers and now and again setting one alight and burning it to the bitter end.

At last James could keep his seat no longer, and begged my permission to be so unmannerly as to walk about. "I am but poor company altogether, sir," says he. "I can think of nothing but this dreadful accident, and the trouble it is like to bring upon quite innocent persons." A little after he observed his son burning a paper which he thought should have been kept, and in the outburst of his excitement he struck the lad repeatedly.

"Are you gone mad?" he cried. "Do you wish to hang your father?" The young man answered nothing, only the wife, at the name of hanging, threw her apron over her face and sobbed louder than before.

This was wretched for a stranger to hear and see, and I was right glad when Alan returned in his fine French clothes, though they were now grown almost too battered to deserve the name of fine. I was then taken out by another of the sons, and given that change of clothing which I had so long needed.

By the time I came back it seemed understood that I was to fly with Alan. They gave us each a sword and pistols (though I professed my inability to use the former); and with these, and some ammunition, a bag of oatmeal, an iron pan, and a bottle of brandy, we were ready for the heather. Money, indeed, was lacking. I had about two guineas. Alan, his belt having been dispatched by another hand, had no more than seventeen pence to his whole fortune, and James, it appears, had brought himself so low with legal expenses on behalf of the tenants, that he could only scrape together three-and-fivepence-halfpenny.

"This'll no do," said Alan.

"Ye must find a safe bit somewhere nearby," said James, "and get word sent to me. This is no time to be stayed for a guinea or two. They're sure to seek ye and to lay on ye the blame of this day's accident. If it falls on you, it falls on me that am your kinsman and harbored ye. And if it comes on me—" he paused, and bit his fingers "—it would be a painful thing for our friends if I was to hang."

"It would be an ill day for Appin," says Alan.

"Well," said James, "ye'll see that I'll have to get a paper out against ye mysel'; I'll have to offer a reward for ye! It's a sore thing to do between such near friends, but I'll have to fend for myself, man. Do ye see that?" He spoke with a pleading earnestness, taking Alan by the breast of the coat.

"Ay," said Alan, "I see that."

"And ye'll have to be clear of the country, Alan—ay, clear of Scotland—you and your friend from the Lowlands, too. For I'll have to paper your friend!"

I thought Alan flushed a bit. "This is unco hard on me that brought him here, James," said he, throwing his head back. "It's like making me a traitor!"

"Now, Alan, man!" cried James. "Look things in the face! Mungo Campbell'll be sure to paper him. What matters if I paper him too? Just the habit Mungo saw him in and what he looked like."

"There's one thing," said Alan, "naebody kens his name." He turned to me. "Well, sir, what say ye to that? Ye are here under the safeguard of my honor. It's my part to see nothing done but what shall please you."

"To all this dispute I am a perfect stranger," said I, "but the plain common sense is to set the blame on the man that fired the shot. Paper him and let innocent folk show their faces in safety."

At this both Alan and James cried out in horror, asking me what the Camerons would think (which confirmed it must have been a Cameron that did the act), and if I did not see that the lad might be caught?

They spoke with such earnestness that I despaired of argument. "Very well, paper me, paper Alan, paper King George! We're all three innocent, and that seems to be what's wanted. But at least, sir," said I to James, "I am Alan's friend, and if I can be helpful to friends of his, I will not stumble at the risk."

I thought it best to put a fair face on my consent, for I saw Alan troubled. I had no sooner said the words than Mrs. Stewart came running over to us, and wept first upon Alan's neck and then on mine, blessing God for our goodness to her family. "As for you, my lad," she says, "my heart is sad not to have your name, but I have your face; and as long as my heart beats under my bosom, I will keep it and think of it." With that she kissed me, and burst once more into sobbing.

"Hoot, hoot," said Alan, looking mighty silly. "The day comes unco soon, and tomorrow there'll be a fine riding of dragoons and running of redcoats in Appin. It behoves you and me to be gone."

Thereupon we said farewell, and set out again, bending eastwards, in the mild dark night.

CHAPTER XII

The flight in the heather and the Heugh of Corrynakiegh

SOMETIMES WE WALKED, SOMETIMES RAN. Though the country appeared desolate, we came now and then to huts and houses of the people, hidden in the quiet places of the hills. Alan would rap upon the side of a house and pass the news to some awakened sleeper at the window. This was so much of a duty in that country, that Alan must pause to attend to it even while fleeing for his life.

So for all our hurry, day began to come in while we were still far from any shelter. It found us in a rock-strewn valley below wild mountains where ran a foaming river and where grew neither grass nor trees (I have thought since that it may have been the valley called Glencoe). I could see Alan knit his brow. "This is no fit place for you and me," he said. "This is a place they're bound to watch."

And with that he ran harder than ever down to the waterside, where the river was split in two by rocks. It went through with a horrid thundering that made my belly quake; and over the river hung a mist of spray. Alan jumped clean upon the middle rock and fell there on his hands and knees to check himself. I had scarce time to measure the distance or to understand the peril before I had followed him, and he had caught and stopped me.

So there we stood, side by side upon a small rock slippery with spray, a far broader leap in front of us, and the river dinning upon all sides. There came on me a deadly sickness of fear, and I put my hand over my eyes. Alan shook me, and I saw that he was speaking, and that his face was red with anger, but the roaring of the falls prevented me from hearing. The same look showed me the water raging by, so that I covered my eyes again and shuddered.

The next minute Alan set the brandy bottle to my lips and forced me to drink a little, which sent the blood into my head again. Then, putting his mouth to my ear, he shouted, "Hang or drown!" and turning his back upon me, leaped over the farther branch of the stream, and landed safe. The brandy was singing in my ears. I had his good example fresh before me, and just wit enough to see that if I did not leap at once, I should never leap at all. I bent low on my knees and flung myself forth, with that kind of anger of despair that has sometimes stood me in stead of courage. Sure enough, only my hands reached the full length. These slipped and I was sliddering into the torrent, when Alan seized me and dragged me into safety.

Never a word he said, but set off running again, and I must stagger to my feet and run after him. I had been weary before, but now I was sick and bruised, and partly drunken with the brandy. I kept stumbling; I had a stitch that came near to overmaster me; and when at last Alan paused under a great rock, it was none too soon for David Balfour.

By rights it was two rocks leaning together at the top, both some twenty feet high, and at the first sight inaccessible. It was only at the third trial, and then by standing on my shoulders and leaping up with such force as I thought must have broken my collarbone, that Alan secured a lodgment. Once there, he let down his leathern girdle and I scrambled up beside him.

The dawn had come quite clear and I could see why we had come there. The two rocks, being hollow on top and sloping one to the other, made a kind of saucer, where as many as four men might have hidden.

At last Alan smiled. "Ay," said he, "now we have a chance." Then he looked at me with some amusement. "Ye're no very brisk at jumping," said he. I colored with mortification and he added at once, "Small blame to ye! To be feared of a thing and yet to do it is what makes the prettiest kind of a man. It's no you that's to blame, it's me."

I asked him why.

"Why," said he, "I have proved myself a gomeral this night. First I take a wrong road in my own country of Appin so that the day has caught us where we should never have been. And next I have come wanting a water bottle, and here we lie for a long summer's day with naething but neat spirit. Before night comes, David, ye'll give me news of that."

Anxious to redeem my character, I offered, if he would pour out the brandy, to fill the bottle at the river.

"I wouldnae waste the good spirit," says he. "What's mair, ye may have observed that Alan Breck Stewart was perhaps walking quicker than his ordinar'."

"You!" I cried. "You were running fit to burst."

"Was I so?" said he. "Then ye may depend there was nae time to be lost. Now gang you to sleep, lad. I'll watch."

Accordingly, I lay down. A little peaty earth had drifted between the top of the two rocks, and some bracken grew there, to be a bed to me. The last thing I heard was the crying of eagles round a cliff at the edge of the valley.

Late in the morning I was roughly awakened, and found Alan's hand pressed upon my mouth. "Wheesht! Ye were snoring," he whispered, and signed to me to peer over the edge of the rock.

The sun was high and very hot, and the valley was as clear as in a picture. Half a mile up the water was a camp of redcoats. A big fire blazed in their midst, at which some were cooking; and nearby, on the top of a rock as high as ours, there stood a sentry, with the sun sparkling on his arms. All along the riverside were posted sentries; higher up the glen, where the ground was more open, the chain of posts was continued by horse soldiers, riding to and fro. I took but one look and ducked again into my place.

"Ye see," said Alan, "I was afraid that they would watch this burnside. They began to come in about two hours ago. If they get up the hill they could easy spy us, but if they keep in the foot of the valley, we'll do yet. The posts are thinner down the water. Come night, we'll try our hand at getting by them."

"And what are we to do till night?" I asked.

"Lie here," says he, "and birstle."

That one good Scotch word, "birstle," was indeed the story of the day. We lay on the top of the rock, like scones upon a griddle. The sun beat upon us cruelly. The rock grew so heated a man could scarce endure the touch of it, and the little patch of earth and fern, which kept cooler, was only large enough for one at a time. We had only raw brandy to drink, which was worse than nothing. But we kept the bottle as cool as we could, burying it in the earth, and got some relief by bathing our breasts and temples.

The soldiers kept stirring all day, in patrolling parties hunting among the rocks. We could see them pike their bayonets among the heather, which sent a cold thrill through my vitals. One fellow actually clapped his hand upon the face of the rock on which we lay, and plucked it off again with an oath. "I tell you it's 'ot," said he; it was the first time I had heard actual English speech and I was amazed at the clipping tones, the odd singsong, and that strange trick of dropping the letter *h*.

The tediousness and pain of being upon the rock grew greater as the day went on. At last, about two, it was beyond men's bearing and, the sun being got a little into the west, a patch of shade came on the east side of our rock, which was sheltered from the soldiers.

"As well one death as another," said Alan, and slipped over the edge and dropped on the ground on the shadowy side. I followed him and instantly fell all my length, so weak was I with that long exposure. Here, then, we lay quite naked to the eye of any soldier who should have strolled that way. None came, however, and after an hour or two we began to get a little strength. As the soldiers, having searched this side of the valley, were now lying closer along the riverside, Alan proposed that we should try a start. So we began to slip from rock to rock, down the valley and towards the mountains, now crawling flat on our bellies in the shade, now making a run for it, heart in mouth.

We drew steadily away, but the business was the most wearing I had ever known. A man had need of a hundred eyes in every part of him, to keep concealed in that uneven country and within cry of so many scattered sentries. When we must pass an open place, quickness was not all, but a swift judgment of the lie of the country and every stone on which we must set foot. The afternoon was now so breathless that the rolling of a pebble sounded like a pistol shot, and would start the echo calling among the hills and cliffs.

By sundown, when we had made some distance, we came on something that put all fears out of season, and that was a deep rushing burn that tore down to join the glen river. We cast ourselves on the ground and plunged head and shoulders in the water, and I cannot tell which was the more pleasant, the great shock as the cool stream went over us, or the greed with which we drank of it. The banks hid us there and at last, being wonderfully renewed, we got out the meal bag and made drammach in the iron pan. (This is but cold water mingled with oatmeal, yet it makes a good enough dish for a man where there are reasons for not making fire, and it is the standby of those who have taken to the heather.)

As soon as the night had fallen, we set forth again, at first with the same caution, but presently standing our full height and stepping out at a good pace, though the way now lay up the steep sides of mountains and along the brows of cliffs. The moon shone out in its last quarter, and presently we saw it reflected far underneath us on the narrow arm of a sea loch.

At this sight Alan paused to make sure of his direction. Seemingly he was well pleased, and he must certainly have judged us out of earshot of our enemies, for hereafter he beguiled the way with whistling many tunes that made the foot go faster. At dawn we reached our destination, a cleft in the head of a great mountain, with a water running through the midst, and upon the one hand a shallow cave in a rock.

The name of the cleft was the Heugh of Corrynakiegh. Although from its height, it was often beset with clouds, it was a pleasant place for the five days we lived in it. Birches and pines grew there in a pretty wood. The burn was full of trout, the wood of cushat doves, and on the open side of the mountain beyond, whaups, or large curlews, would be always whistling.

From the cleft we looked down at a great height upon Loch Leven, which divides Appin from Mamore, north across the water. We slept in the cave, making our bed of heather and covering ourselves with Alan's greatcoat. There was a concealed place in the glen, where we were so bold as to make fire so that we could cook porridge, and grill the little trouts that we caught with our hands under the overhanging banks of the burn. Indeed, with a rivalry that much amused us, we spent a great part of our days at the waterside, groping about or, as they say, guddling for these fish.

In any by-time Alan must teach me to use my sword. My ignorance had much distressed him but he made it more of a pain than need have been, for he stormed at me all through the lessons in a very violent manner. I was often tempted to turn tail, but held my ground for all that and got some profit of my lessons; if it was but to stand on guard with an assured countenance, which is often all that is required.

Meanwhile, you are not to suppose that we neglected our chief business, which was to get away. On our first morning, Alan said, "Now we must somehow get word to James, and he must find the siller for us." Thereupon he fell in a muse, looking into the embers of the fire. Presently, he fashioned two pieces of wood into a cross, the four ends of which he blackened on the coals. Then he looked at me shyly. "Could ye lend me my button?" says he. "It seems strange to ask a gift again, but I own I am laith to cut another."

I gave him the button. He strung it on a strip of his greatcoat which he had used to bind the cross and tied in a sprig of birch and another of fir.

"Now," said he with satisfaction, "there is a little clachan [a hamlet] not far from here, named Koalisnacoan, where there are many friends whom I could trust with my life and some that I am no so sure of. See, David, there will be money set upon our heads, and I would as lief they didnae see me. There's bad folk everywhere, and what's worse, weak ones. So when it comes dark, I will steal into that hamlet and set this cross in the window of a good friend of mine, John Breck Maccoll, a tenant of Appin's."

"And if he finds it, what is he to think?" says I.

"This cross," says Alan, "is something in the nature of the cross-tarrie, which is the signal of gathering in our clans. Yet he will know the clan is not to rise, for there is no word with it. So he will say to himsel', 'The clan is not to rise, but there is something.' Then he will see my button and he will say, 'The son of Duncan Stewart is in the heather, and has need of me.'"

"It may be," says I. "But there is a good deal of heather between here and the Forth."

"That is true," says Alan. "But then John Breck will see the sprigs of birch and pine and he will think to himsel' (if he is a man of any penetration), 'Alan will be lying in a wood of pines and birches. That is not so very rife hereabout.' Then he will give us a look up in Corrynakiegh. And if he does not, David, the devil may fly away with him; for he will no be worth the salt to his porridge."

"Eh, man," said I, drolling with him a little, "you're very ingenious! But would it not be simpler to write a few words in black and white?"

"It would certainly be much simpler for me to write," says Alan. "But it would be a sore job for John Breck to read it. He would have to go to school for two–three years, and it's possible we might be wearied waiting on him."

So that night Alan carried down his crosstarrie and set it in the tenant's window. The next day we lay in the borders of the wood and kept a close lookout for John Breck.

About noon a man was to be spied, straggling up the open mountainside in the sun, looking round him as he came. Alan whistled. The man turned and came a little towards us. Then Alan would give another "Peep!" And so, by the sound of whistling, the man was guided to the spot where we lay.

He was a ragged, wild, bearded man, about forty, and disfigured with the smallpox. His English was very bad and broken, and perhaps this made him appear more backward than he really was, but I thought he had little good will to serve us.

Alan would have had him tell our message to James, but he would forget it, he said, and would either have a letter or wash his hands of us.

I thought Alan would be graveled for the means of writing. But he was a man of more resources than I knew; he searched the wood until he found a quill of a cushat dove, which he shaped into a pen; he made himself a kind of ink with gunpowder and water, and tearing a corner from his French military commission (which he carried like a talisman to keep him from the gallows), he wrote as follows:

Dear Kinsman,—Please send the money by the bearer to the place he kens.   Your affectionate cousin, A. S.

This he entrusted to the tenant, who promised to make what speed he could, and carried it off with him down the hill.

He was three full days gone, but about five in the evening of the third we heard a whistling in the wood, which Alan answered, and presently the tenant came up the waterside. He gave us news that the country was alive with redcoats. Arms were being found, and poor folk brought in trouble daily. James and some of his servants were already clapped in prison at Fort William, under strong suspicion of complicity. It seemed it was noised on all sides that Alan

81

Breck had fired the shot; and there was a bill issued for both him and me, with one hundred pounds reward.

This was all as bad as could be, and the little note the tenant had carried us from Mrs. Stewart was also of a miserable sadness. In it she assured Alan, if he fell into the hands of the troops, both he and James were no better than dead men. The money she had sent was all that she could beg or borrow. Lastly, she said, she enclosed one of the bills in which we were described.

This we looked upon with great curiosity, partly as a man may look in a mirror, partly as he might look into the barrel of an enemy's gun to judge if it be truly aimed. Alan was well enough pleased to see his finery fully set down. Only when he came to the words, "a blue French side-coat with silver buttons and lace a great deal tarnished," he looked a little mortified. As for myself, I cut a miserable figure in the bill and yet I too was well enough pleased, for since I had changed my rags, the description had ceased to be a danger and become a source of safety.

"Alan," said I, "you should change your clothes."

"Na, troth!" said Alan. "I have nae others. A fine sight I would be, if I went back to France in a bonnet!"

This put a second reflection in my mind: that if I were to separate from the reputed murderer, and his telltale clothes, I should be safe against arrest, and might go openly about my business. For generosity's sake, I dared not speak my mind upon this, but I thought of it all the more when the tenant brought out only four guineas in gold. True, it was more than I had, but Alan had to get as far as France; I, with my less than two guineas, not beyond Queensferry. So, taking things in their proportion, Alan's society was not only a peril to my life, but a burden on my purse.

But there was no thought of the sort in the honest head of my companion. He believed he was helping and protecting me. "It's little enough," said he, putting the guineas in his purse, "but it'll do my business. And now, John Breck, if ye will hand me my button, this gentleman and me will be for taking the road."

The tenant handed the button to Alan, who gave it to me, and said, "Here is my button back, and I thank you for parting with it, which is of a piece with all your friendships to me." Then he took the warmest parting of the tenant. "For," says he, "ye have done well by me, and set your neck at a venture, and I will always give you the name of a good man."

Lastly, the tenant took himself off by one way; and Alan and I, getting our chattels together, struck into another to resume our flight.

CHAPTER XIII

The flight in the heather continued and Cluny's Cage

MORE THAN ELEVEN HOURS of incessant, hard traveling brought us early next morning to the end of a mountain range. In front of us there lay a piece of low, deserted land. The sun, not long up, shone straight in our eyes, and a thin mist went up from the moorland like smoke, so that as Alan said there might have been twenty squadron of dragoons there and we none the wiser. We sat down, therefore, till the mist should have risen, and made ourselves a dish of drammach, and held a council of war.

"David," said Alan, "this is the kittle bit. Appin's fair death to us. To the south it's all Campbells. There's no muckle to be gained by going north, neither for you, that wants to get to Queensferry, nor for me, that wants to get to France. We can strike east."

"East be it!" says I cheerily, but I was thinking to myself: If you would only take one point of the compass, and let me take any other, it would be best for us both.

"Well, then, east," said Alan. "But once on yon naked, flat place, where can a body turn to? The redcoats can spy you miles away. And I'm free to say, it's worse by daylight than by dark. Shall we risk it and stave on ahead?"

"Alan," said I, "it's all a risk. We have none too much money, nor yet meal. The longer they seek, the nearer they may guess where we are. I give my word to go ahead until we drop."

Alan was delighted. "There are whiles," said he, "when ye are altogether too canny and Whiggish to be company for a gentleman like me; then other whiles ye show yoursel' a mettle spark, and it's then, David, that I love ye like a brother."

The mist rose and showed us that country lying as waste as the sea; only the moorfowl and the peewees crying upon it, and far over to the east a herd of deer, moving like dots. It was red with heather, broken up with bogs and peaty pools, and in one place there was a forest of dead firs, standing like skeletons. But at least it was clear of troops.

So we went down, and began to make our devious travels towards the eastern verge of the moor. There were the mountain-tops all round from whence we might be spied at any moment, so it behoved us to keep in the hollows, and when these turned aside from our direction, to move upon the naked moor with infinite care. Sometimes, for half an hour, we must crawl from one heather bush to another, as hunters do when they are hard upon the deer.

It was a clear day again, with a blazing sun, and the water in the brandy bottle was soon gone. Toiling and resting and toiling again, we wore away the morning, and about noon lay down in a thick bush of heather to sleep. Alan took the first watch and it seemed to me I had scarce closed my eyes before I was shaken up to take the second. We had no clock to go by. Instead, Alan stuck a sprig of heath in the ground so that as soon as the shadow of the bush should fall so far to the east, I might know to rouse him. But I was so weary that my joints slept even when my mind was waking. The hot smell of heather and the drone of the bees were like possets to me, and every now and again I would give a jump and find I had been dozing.

The last time I woke I thought the sun had taken a great start in the heavens. I looked at the sprig of heath and I could have cried aloud, for I had betrayed my trust. My head was nearly turned with fear and shame and, when I looked around me on the moor, my heart was like dying in my body. Sure enough, a body of horse soldiers were drawing near to us from the southeast, spread out in the shape of a fan.

When I waked Alan, he glanced first at the soldiers, then at the mark and the position of the sun, and knitted his brows with a sudden, anxious look, which was all the reproach I had of him.

"What are we to do now?" I asked.

"We'll have to play at being hares," said he. "Do ye see yon mountain?" pointing to one on the northeastern sky. "Its name is Ben Alder. It is full of hills and hollows, and if we can win to it before the morn, we may do yet."

"But, Alan," cried I, "that will take us across the coming of the soldiers!"

"I ken that fine," said he, "but if we are driven back on Appin, we are two dead men. So now, David man, be brisk!"

With that he began to go forward on his hands and knees with an incredible quickness, winding in and out in the lower parts of the moorland, where we were the best concealed. Some of these had been scathed with a heath fire, and there rose in our faces a blinding, choking dust as fine as smoke.

Now and then, where there was a big bush of heather, we lay awhile panting and looking back at the dragoons. They had not spied us, for they held straight on; a half troop covering and beating about two miles of ground. Even as it was, the least misfortune might still betray us, and now and again, when a grouse rose out of the heather with a clap of wings, we lay as still as the dead and were afraid to breathe.

The aching of my body, the laboring of my heart, the soreness of my hands, and the smarting of my throat and eyes in the dust had grown so unbearable that nothing but the fear of Alan lent me enough false courage to continue. As for himself (and you are to bear in mind that he was cumbered with a greatcoat), he had first turned crimson, but as time went on the redness mingled with patches of white, and his breath cried and whistled. Yet he seemed in no way dashed in spirits and I was driven to marvel at the man's endurance.

At length, in the first gloaming of the night, we heard a trumpet sound, and looking back, saw the troop collecting. A little after, they had built a fire and camped. At this I begged that we might lie down and sleep.

"There shall be no sleep the night!" said Alan. "Tomorrow, these dragoons will keep the crown of the muirland. None will get out of Appin but winged fowls. Na, na, when the day comes, it shall find you and me in a fast place on Ben Alder."

"Alan," I said, "it's not the want of will: it's the strength that I want. If I could, I would; but I cannot."

"Very well, then," said Alan. "I'll carry ye."

I looked to see if he were jesting, but the little man was in dead earnest, and the sight of so much resolution shamed me. "Lead away," said I. "I'll follow."

He gave me one look as much as to say, "Well done, David!" and off he set again at his top speed.

It grew cooler and a little darker with the coming of night. (In the darkest part of those nights so far north you would have needed good eyes to read, but for all that, I have often seen it darker in a winter midday.) Heavy dew drenched the moor, and refreshed me. When we stopped to breathe, and I had time to see all about me the clearness and sweetness of the night, the shapes of the hills like things asleep, and the soldiers' fire dwindling away behind us, anger would come upon me that I must still drag myself in agony and eat the dust like a worm.

But day began to come in, after years, I thought; and by that time we were past the greatest danger, and could walk upon our feet like men, instead of crawling like brutes. But what a pair we must have made, going double like grandfathers, stumbling like babes, and as white as dead folk. Never a word passed between us. Each set his mouth and kept his eyes in front of him.

Alan, it is plain, must have been as stupid with weariness as myself, and looked as little where we were going, or we should not have walked into an ambush like blind men.

We were going down a brae, Alan leading and I following a pace or two behind, when upon a sudden the heather rustled, four ragged men leaped out, and the next moment we were lying on our backs, with dirks at our throats.

I was too glad to have stopped walking to mind about a dirk, and the pain of this rough handling was quite swallowed up by the pains of which I was already full. The face of the man that held me down was black with the sun and his eyes very light, but I was not afraid of him. I heard Alan and another whispering in Gaelic, and what they said was all one to me.

Then the dirks were put up, our weapons were taken away, and we were set face to face, sitting in the heather. "They are Cluny's outsentries," said Alan. "We couldnae have fallen better. We're just to bide here till they get word to the chief of my arrival."

Now Cluny Macpherson had been one of the leaders of the great rebellion six years before. There was a price on his life, and I had supposed him long ago in France. "What," I cried, "is Cluny still here?"

"Ay, still in his own country and kept by his own clan," said Alan, and without more words, he rolled on his face in deep heather, and seemed to sleep at once.

No such thing was possible for me. I had no sooner closed my eyes than my head and body seemed to be filled with whirring grasshoppers, and I must tumble and toss, and look at the dazzling sky, or at Cluny's wild, dirty sentries.

At last, the messenger returned. Cluny would be glad to receive us. We must set forward once more. Alan was in excellent spirits, refreshed by his sleep, and looking forward to a dram and a dish of venison collops, of which the messenger had brought him word. For my part, it made me sick to hear of eating. I had been dead-heavy before, now I felt like a gossamer. The ground seemed a cloud, the air a current, which carried me to and fro. I remember that I could not stop smiling, hard as I tried.

I saw Alan knitting his brows at me, and supposed it was in anger, but my good companion had nothing in his mind but kindness. The next moment, two of the gillies had me by the arms and I was carried with great swiftness (or so it appeared to me) through a labyrinth of dreary glens into the heart of Ben Alder.

We came at last to the foot of an exceeding steep wood which scrambled up a craggy hillside, and was crowned by a precipice.

"It's here," said one of the guides, and we struck uphill. The trees clung upon the slope like sailors on the shrouds of a ship, and their trunks were like the rounds of a ladder, by which we mounted. At the top, just before the rocky cliff face sprang above the foliage, we found the strange house, which was known in that country as Cluny's Cage. The trunks of several trees had been wattled across, the intervals strengthened with stakes, and the ground behind this barricade leveled up with earth to make the floor. A tree, which grew out from the hillside, was the living centerbeam of the roof. The walls were of wattle and covered with moss. The whole house had something of an egg shape. It half hung, half stood in that steep, hillside thicket, like a wasp's nest in a green hawthorn.

Within, it was large enough to shelter five or six persons with comfort. A projection of the cliff had been cunningly employed as the fireplace, so that the smoke, rising against the similar color of the face of the rock, readily escaped notice from below.

When we came to the door, Cluny was seated by this chimney, watching a gillie about some cookery. He was plainly habited, with a knitted nightcap over his ears, and smoked a foul pipe. For all that, he had the manners of a king.

"Well, Mr. Stewart, come awa', sir," said he, rising out of his place to welcome us, "and bring in your friend."

"And how is yourself, Cluny?" said Alan. "I am proud to see ye, and to present my friend the Laird of Shaws, Mr. David Balfour."

"I make ye welcome," says Cluny. "My house is a queer, rude place, but one where I have entertained a royal personage, Mr. Stewart—ye doubtless ken the personage I have in my eye. We'll take a dram for luck, and as soon as the collops are ready, we'll dine, and take a hand at the cartes as gentlemen should. My life is a bit driegh," says he, pouring out the brandy. "I sit and twirl my thumbs, and mind upon a great day that is gone by, and weary for another that we all hope will be upon the road. So here's a toast: The Restoration!"

We all touched glasses and drank. I am sure I wished no ill to King George, and if he had been there himself, it's like he would have done as I did. No sooner had I taken the dram than I felt hugely better, and could look on and listen.

Certainly, we had a strange host. In his long hiding, Cluny had grown to have the precise habits of an old maid. He had a particular place, where no one else must sit. The Cage was arranged in a particular way, which none must disturb. Cookery was one of his chief fancies, and even while he was greeting us, he kept an eye on the collops.

It appears he sometimes visited or received visits from his wife and nearest friends under cover of night, but for the more part communicated only with his sentinels and the gillies that waited on him. First thing in the morning, one of them, who was a barber, came and shaved him, and gave him the news of the country, of which he was immoderately greedy. Disputes were brought to him, for he still exercised a patriarchal justice in his clan; and his men, who would have snapped their fingers at the Court of Session, laid aside revenge and paid down money at his bare word. When he was angered, which was often enough, he gave commands and breathed threats of punishment like any king. With each of his gillies, as he entered, he ceremoniously shook hands, both parties touching their bonnets in a military manner. Altogether, I had a fair chance to see the inner workings of a Highland clan; and this when the least of the ragged fellows whom he rated and threatened could have made a fortune by betraying their fugitive chief.

On that first day, as soon as the collops were ready, Cluny bade us draw in to our meal. "The collops," said he, "are such as I gave his Royal Highness in this very house," and Cluny entertained us with stories of Prince Charlie's stay in the Cage, giving us the words of the speakers, and rising to show us where they stood.

We were no sooner done eating than Cluny brought out a thumbed, greasy pack of cards, and his eyes brightened as he proposed that we should play. Now I had been brought up by my father to eschew gambling like disgrace. To be sure, I might have pleaded fatigue, which was excuse enough; but I thought that I should bear a testimony, and, red in the face, I told them I had no call to judge others, but for my own part, it was a matter in which I had no clearness.

Cluny stopped mingling the cards. "What kind of Whiggish, canting talk is this, for the house of Cluny Macpherson?" says he.

"I will put my hand in the fire for Mr. Balfour," says Alan, cocking his hat. "I bear a king's name, and I and any that I call friend are company for the best. But the gentleman is tired, and should sleep. If he has no mind to the cartes, it will never hinder you and me."

"Sir," says Cluny, "in this house I would have you ken that any gentleman may follow his pleasure. If your friend would like to stand on his head, he is welcome. And if either he, or you, is not preceesely satisfied, I will be proud to step outside with him."

I had no will that these two friends should cut their throats for my sake. "Sir," said I, "I am wearied, as Alan says. What's more, as you are a man that likely has sons of your own, I may tell you it was a promise to my father."

"Say nae mair," said Cluny, and pointed me to a bed of heather in a corner. For all that he was displeased enough but, what with the brandy and venison, heaviness had come over me. I had scarce lain down before I fell into a kind of trance, in which I continued almost the whole time of our stay in the Cage.

Sometimes I was awake and understood what passed. Sometimes I only heard voices. I must sometimes have cried out, for I remember I was now and then amazed at being answered. The barber-gillie, who was a doctor too, was called in to prescribe for me. I knew well enough that I was ill, but he spoke in Gaelic, and I was too sick to ask for a translation of his opinion.

While I lay in this poor pass, Alan and Cluny were most of the time at the cards. I am clear that Alan must have begun by winning, for I remember seeing a great glittering pile of as much as a hundred guineas on the table. Even then, I thought it seemed deep water for Alan to be riding, who had no better battle horse than a matter of four pounds.

The luck changed on the second day. About noon I was awakened and given as usual a dram with some bitter infusion which the barber had prescribed. The sun, shining in at the open door of the Cage, dazzled and offended me. Cluny sat at the table, biting the pack of cards. Alan had stopped over the bed, and had his face close to my eyes. He asked me for a loan of my money.

"But why?" said I. "I don't see."

"Hut, David," said Alan, "ye wouldnae grudge me a loan?"

I would though, if I had had my senses! But all I thought of then was to get his face away, and I handed him my money.

On the morning of the third day, I awoke with a great relief of spirits, very weak and weary, but seeing things with their honest everyday appearance. I had a mind to eat, moreover, rose from bed of my own movement, and as soon as I had breakfasted, stepped outside the Cage. It was a gray, mild day, and I sat in a dream all morning at the top of the wood.

When I returned, Cluny and Alan had laid the cards aside, and were questioning a gillie. The chief turned and spoke to me in Gaelic.

"I have no Gaelic, sir," said I.

Now since the card question, everything I said or did had the power of annoying Cluny. "Your name has more sense than yourself, then," said he, angrily; "for it's good Gaelic. But the point is this. My scout reports all clear in the south, and the question is, have ye the strength to go?"

I saw cards on the table, but no gold; only a heap of little written papers, all on Cluny's side. I began to have strong misgivings.

"I do not know if I am as well as I should be," said I, looking at Alan, "but the little money we have has a long way to carry us."

Alan took his underlip into his mouth and looked upon the ground. "David," says he at last, "I've lost it. There's the truth. Ye shouldnae have given your money to me. I'm daft when I get to the cartes."

"Of course you'll have your money back," cried Cluny. "It's not to be supposed that I would be any hindrance to gentlemen in your situation." And he began to pull gold out of his pocket with a mighty red face.

Alan said nothing, only looked on the ground.

"Will you step to the door with me, sir?" said I.

Cluny said he would be very glad, and followed me readily

enough, but he looked flustered and put out. "And now, sir," says I, "I must first acknowledge your generosity."

"Nonsense!" cries Cluny. "This is just a most unfortunate affair. But what would ye have me do—boxed up in this cage of mine—but just set my friends to the cartes, when I can get them? And if they lose, of course, it's not to be supposed—"

"Yes," said I, "if they lose, you give them back their money: and if they win, they carry away yours in their pouches! I have said before that I grant your generosity, sir, but it's a very painful thing to be placed in this position."

There was a little silence, in which Cluny grew redder and redder in the face.

"So you see, sir," said I, "there is something to be said upon my side. This gambling is a very poor employ for gentlefolks. But I am a young man and I ask your advice. My friend fairly lost this money. Can I accept it back again? Would that be the right part for me to play? Whatever I do, you can see for yourself it must be hard upon a man of any pride."

Cluny looked me over with a warlike eye. But either my youth disarmed him, or perhaps his own sense of justice. "Mr. Balfour," said he, "I think you are too covenanting, but you have the spirit of a very pretty gentleman. Upon my honest word, ye may take this money—it's what I would tell my own son—and here's my hand along with it!"

CHAPTER XIV

The quarrel

UNDER CLOUD OF NIGHT Alan and I were put across Loch Errocht, which lay below Ben Alder, and led by one of Cluny's gillies to another hiding place near the head of Loch Rannoch. This fellow carried all our luggage, and perhaps without that relief I could not have walked at all. I was but new arisen from a bed of sickness, and there was nothing in the state of our affairs to hearten me, traveling, as we did, over the most dismal deserts in Scotland, under a cloudy heaven, and with divided hearts.

For long, we said nothing: each marching with a set countenance; I, angry and proud; Alan, ashamed that he had lost my money and angry that I should take it so ill.

The thought of a separation ran stronger in my mind; and the more I approved of it, the more ashamed I grew of my approval. It would be a handsome, generous thing for Alan to turn round and say to me: "Go. My company only increases your danger." But for me to turn to the friend who certainly loved me, and say: "Your friendship is a burden. Go take your risks alone—" was impossible.

Yet Alan had behaved like a treacherous child. Wheedling my money from me while I lay half-conscious was scarce better than theft; and here he was trudging by my side, without a penny to his name, quite blithe to sponge upon the money he had driven me to beg. True, I was ready to share it with him, but it made me rage to see him count upon my readiness. So I said nothing, nor so much as looked at him, save with the tail of my eye.

At last, upon the other side of Loch Errocht, going over a smooth, rushy place where the walking was easy, he could bear it no longer, and came close to me. "David," says he, "this is no way for two friends to take a small accident. I say that I'm sorry. And now if you have anything, ye'd better say it."

"O," says I, "I have nothing."

"But when I say I was to blame?" said he, with a trembling voice.

"Why, of course, ye were to blame," said I, coolly; "and you will bear me out that I have never reproached you."

"Never," says he; "but ye ken very well that ye've done worse. Are we to part? Ye said so once before. Are ye to say it again? I own I'm no very keen to stay where I'm no wanted."

This pierced me like a sword, and seemed to lay bare my private disloyalty. "Alan Breck!" I cried. "Do you think I am one to turn my back on you in your chief need? My whole conduct's there to give the lie to it. It's true. I fell asleep upon the muir, but that was from weariness, and you do wrong to cast it up to me—"

"Which is what I never did," said Alan.

"Aside from that," I continued, "I never yet failed a friend. It's not likely I'll begin with you. There are things between us that I can never forget, even if you can."

"I will only say this, David," said Alan, very quietly. "I have long been owing ye my life. Now I owe ye money. Ye should try to make that burden light for me."

This ought to have touched me, and it did, but in the wrong manner. I felt I was behaving badly; and was now not only angry with Alan, but angry with myself in the bargain.

"You asked me to speak," said I. "Well, then, I will. You own yourself that you have done me a disservice. I have never reproached you. And now you blame me because I cannae laugh and sing as if I was glad to be affronted. The next thing will be that I'm to go down upon my knees and thank you for it! Ye should think more of others, Alan Breck. When a friend has passed over an offense without a word, you should let it lie, instead of making it a stick to break his back."

"Aweel," said Alan, "say nae mair."

We fell back into our former silence; came to our journey's end, supped, and lay down to sleep, without another word.

The next day the gillie put us across Loch Rannoch, and gave us his opinion as to our best route to the Lowlands. Alan was little pleased with this route, which led us through the mountainous country of his blood foes, the Glenorchy Campbells. But the gillie, who was the chief of Cluny's scouts, had good reasons to give on all hands, naming the force of troops in every district, and alleging we should nowhere be so little troubled as in a country of the Campbells, and Alan gave way at last. "There's naething in that country but heath, crows, and Campbells," said he. "But I see that ye're a man of penetration, and be it as ye please!"

We set forth accordingly, and for the best part of three nights traveled on eerie mountains and among wild rivers, often buried in mist, almost continually blown and rained upon. By day, we slept in the drenching heather; by night, incessantly clambered upon breakneck hills and among rude crags. A fire was never to be thought of. Our only food was drammach and a portion of cold meat that we had carried from the Cage; and as for drink, Heaven knows we had no want of water. In this almost steady rain the springs of the mountains were broken up and every glen gushed water like a cistern.

This was a dreadful time, and during these horrid wanderings Alan and I had no familiarity, scarcely even that of speech. My best excuse is that I was sickening for my grave, but besides that, I was of an unforgiving disposition from my birth, slow to take offense, slower to forget it. For the best part of two days Alan was unweariedly kind; but I stayed in myself, roughly refusing his services, and passing him over with my eyes as if he had been a bush or a stone.

The peep of the third day found us upon a very open hill, so that we could not follow our usual plan and lie down immediately to eat and sleep. Alan, looking in my face, showed concern. "Ye had better let me take your pack," said he, for perhaps the ninth time since we had parted from the scout.

"I do very well, I thank you," said I, as cold as ice.

Alan flushed darkly. "I'll not offer it again," he said. "I'm not a patient man, David."

"I never said you were," said I, which was exactly the rude, silly speech of a boy of ten.

Alan made no answer at the time, but his conduct answered for him. Henceforth, it is to be thought, he quite forgave himself for the affair at Cluny's; cocked his hat again, walked jauntily, whistled airs, and looked at me with a provoking smile.

The third night we were to pass through Balquhidder. It came clear and cold, and a northerly wind blew the clouds away and made the stars bright. Alan was in high good spirits. As for me, the change of weather came too late. I had lain in the mire so long that (as the Bible has it) my very clothes "abhorred me." I was deadly sick and full of pains and shiverings. The chill of the wind went through me. In this poor state I had to bear a persecution from my companion, who spoke a good deal, and never without a taunt. "Whig" was the best name he had to give me. "Here," he would say, "here's a puddle for ye to jump, my Whiggie! I ken you're a fine jumper!" And so on, all the time gibing.

I knew it was my own doing, but I was too miserable to repent. I felt I could drag myself but little farther. Pretty soon I must lie down and die on these wet mountains like a sheep. My head was light, perhaps, but I began to glory in the prospect of such a death. Alan would repent then, I thought. He would remember, when I was dead, how much he owed me, and the remembrance would be torture. So I went like a silly, bad-hearted schoolboy, when all the while I was growing worse and worse. Flushes of heat went over me, and then spasms of shuddering. The stitch in my side was hardly bearable. At last I began to feel that I could trail myself no farther. There came on me all at once the wish to have it out with Alan and be done with my life. He had just called me "Whig."

I stopped. "Mr. Stewart," said I, in a voice that quivered like a fiddle string, "you are older than I am, and should know your manners. Do you think it wise or witty to cast my politics in my teeth? I thought it was the part of gentlemen to differ civilly."

Alan had stopped opposite me, his hands in his breeches pockets, his head a little on one side. He listened, smiling evilly, as I could see by the starlight. Then he began to whistle, a Jacobite air, made in mockery of the Whigs' defeat at Preston Pans. And it came in my mind that Alan, on the day of that battle, had been engaged upon the royal side.

"Why do ye take that air, Mr. Stewart?" said I. "Is that to remind me you have been beaten on both sides?"

The air stopped on Alan's lips. "David!" said he.

"But it's time these manners ceased," I continued; "and I mean you shall henceforth speak civilly of my King and my good friends the Campbells."

"I am a Stewart—" began Alan.

"O!" says I. "I ken ye bear a king's name. But you have been chased in the field by the grown men of my party. It seems a poor kind of pleasure to outface a boy. You have run before both the Campbells and the Whigs like a hare. It behoves you to speak of them as your betters."

Alan stood quite still, the tails of his greatcoat clapping behind him in the wind. "This is a pity," he said at last. "There are things said that cannot be passed over."

"I never asked you to," said I. "I am as ready as yourself. I am no blower and boaster like some that I could name. Come on!" And drawing my sword, I fell on guard as Alan himself had taught me.

"David!" he cried. "Are ye daft? I cannae draw upon ye, David. It's fair murder."

"That was your lookout when you insulted me," said I.

"It's the truth!" cried Alan, and he stood for a moment in sore perplexity. Then he drew his sword. But before I could touch his blade with mine, he had thrown it from him and fallen to the ground. "Na, na," he kept saying, "I cannae, I cannae."

At this the last of my anger oozed out of me. I would have given the world to take back what I had said. I minded me of all Alan's kindness and courage in the past, and then recalled my own insults. At the same time, the sickness that hung upon me seemed to redouble, and the pang in my side was like a sword. I thought I must have swooned where I stood.

This it was that gave me a thought. No apology could blot out what I had said, but a mere cry for help might bring Alan back to my side. I put my pride away. "Alan," I said, "if you cannae help me, I must just die here." He started up and looked at me. "It's true," said I. "Let me get to a house—I can die there easier." I had no need to pretend. Whether I chose or not, I spoke in a weeping voice that would have melted a heart of stone.

"Can ye walk?" asked Alan.

"No," said I, "not without help. This last hour my legs have been fainting under me, and I cannae breathe right. If I die, ye'll forgive me, Alan? In my heart, I like ye fine—even when I was the angriest."

"Wheesht, wheesht!" cried Alan. "Dinna say that! David man, ye ken—" He shut his mouth upon a sob. "I'm no a right man at all. I have neither sense nor kindness. I couldnae remember ye were just a bairn. I couldnae see you were dying on your feet; Davie, ye'll have to try and forgive me."

"Oh man, let's say no more about it!" said I. "We're neither one of us to mend the other. O, but my stitch is sore. Is there nae house?"

"I'll find a house to ye, David," he said stoutly. "We're in Balquhidder. There should be no want of friends' houses here. We'll follow down the burn. My poor man, will ye no be better on my back?"

"Oh, Alan," says I, "and me a good twelve inches taller?"

"Ye're no such a thing," cried Alan, with a start. "There may be a trifling matter of an inch or two. I'm no saying I'm exactly what ye would call a tall man, whatever, and I daresay," he added, his voice tailing off laughably, "now when I come to think of it, I daresay ye'll be just about right. Ay, it'll be a foot, or may be even mair."

It was sweet to hear Alan eat his words in the fear of some fresh quarrel. I could have laughed had not my stitch caught me so hard, but if I had laughed I think I would have wept too. "Alan," cried I, "what makes ye care for such a thankless fellow?"

"'Deed, and I don't know," said Alan. "For precisely what I thought I liked about ye, was that ye never quarreled; and now I like ye better!"

CHAPTER XV

The end of the flight

AT THE DOOR of the first house we came to, Alan knocked, which was no very safe enterprise in this part of the Highlands. Chance served us very well, for it was a household of Maclarens that we found. The Maclarens followed Alan's chief in war, and made but one clan with Appin, and Alan was not only welcome for his name's sake, but known by reputation. Here I was got to bed without delay, and a doctor fetched, who found me in a sorry plight. But whether because he was a very good doctor, or I a very young, strong man, I lay bedridden for no more than a week, and before a month I was able to take the road again with a good heart.

All this time Alan would not leave me though I often pressed him, and indeed his foolhardiness in staying was a common subject of outcry with the two or three friends that were let into the secret. He hid by day in a hole under a little wood; and at night, when the coast was clear, would visit me. Mrs. Maclaren, our hostess, thought nothing good enough for such a guest, and as Duncan Dhu, our host, had a pair of bagpipes in his house, and was a lover of music, the time of my recovery was quite a festival.

Although my own presence was known before I left to all the people in Balquhidder, the soldiers let us be; and what was more astonishing, no magistrate came near me, and there was no question put of whence I came or whither I was going. Yet the bills in which we were described had now been printed, and Duncan Dhu and those who visited his house could have entertained no doubt of who I was. Other folk keep a secret among two or three near friends, and somehow it leaks out; but among these clansmen it is told to a whole countryside, and they will keep it for a century.

There was but one thing happened worth narrating; and that is the visit I had of Robert Oig Macgregor, one of the sons of the notorious Rob Roy. It was he who had shot one of the Maclarens, a quarrel never satisfied; yet he walked into the house of his blood enemies as a traveler might into a public inn.

Duncan passed me word of who it was, and we looked at one another in concern. It was then close upon the time of Alan's coming, and since Alan took up the quarrel of any relative, however distant, the two were little likely to agree. Yet if we sought to make a signal, it was sure to arouse suspicion in a man under so dark a cloud as Robin Macgregor.

He came in with a great show of civility. But like a man among inferiors, he took off his bonnet to Mrs. Maclaren, then clapped it on his head again to speak to Duncan and to bow to my bedside. Here he made known that he and a relative of mine (of whom I was ashamed to say I knew naught) had been companions-in-arms at Preston Pans, and because of this he had come to bid me well.

This courtesy accomplished, he turned to leave; but while he was still in the door, he met Alan coming in. The two looked at each other like strange dogs. Neither of them were big men, but they seemed fairly to swell out with pride. Each, by a movement, thrust clear the hilt of his sword so that it might be more readily grasped and the blade drawn.

"Mr. Stewart, I am thinking," said Robin. "I did not know ye were in my country, sir."

"It sticks in mind, Mr. Macgregor, that I am in the country of my friends the Maclarens," says Alan.

"That's a kittle point," returned the other. "There may be two words to say to that. But I think I will have heard that you are a man of your sword?"

"Unless ye were born deaf, Mr. Macgregor, ye will have heard a good deal more than that," says Alan. "I am not the only man that can draw steel in Appin. When my kinsman, Ardshiel, had a talk with your father, not so many years back, I could never hear that the Macgregor had the best of it."

"My father was an old man," says Robin. "The match was unequal. You and me would make a better pair, sir."

"I was thinking that," said Alan.

Duncan, who had been hanging at the elbow of these fighting cocks, now thrust himself between them. "Gentlemen," said he, with something of a white face, "I have been thinking of a very different matter. Here are my pipes and here are you two gentlemen, baith acclaimed pipers. It's a braw chance to settle the auld dispute which one of ye's the best."

"Why, sir," said Alan, still addressing Robin, "have ye music, as folk say? Are ye a bit of a piper?"

"I can pipe like a Macrimmon!" cried Robin.

Duncan Dhu made haste to bring out his pipes and to set before his guests a mutton ham and a bottle of that drink called Athole brose, which is made of old whiskey, strained honey and sweet cream. His wife was out of Athole and had a name far and wide for her skill in that confection. The two enemies were still on the very breach of a quarrel, but down they sat, one upon each side of the peat fire, and ate a portion of the ham and drank a glass of the brose to Mrs. Maclaren. Then after a great number of civilities, Robin took the pipes and played a little tune in a very ranting manner.

"Ay, ye can blow," said Alan. Taking the instrument from his rival, he first played the same tune in a manner identical with Robin's; and then wandered into variations decorated with a perfect flight of grace notes, such as pipers love, and call the "warblers."

I had been pleased with Robin's playing; Alan's ravished me.

"That's no very bad, Mr. Stewart," said the rival, "but ye show a poor device in your warblers."

"Me!" cried Alan, the blood starting to his face. "I appeal to Duncan."

"Ye need appeal to naebody," said Robin. "It's God's truth that you're a very creditable piper for a Stewart. Be the judge yourself. Hand me the pipes."

Alan did as he asked. Robin proceeded to imitate and correct Alan's variations, which it seemed that he remembered perfectly. Then he worked them throughout to so new a purpose, with such ingenuity and sentiment, that I was amazed to hear him.

As for Alan, his face grew dark and hot, and he sat and gnawed his fingers. "Enough!" he cried. "Ye can blow the pipes—make the most of that." And he made as if to rise.

But Robin held out his hand for silence, and struck into the slow measure of a pibroch. It was a fine piece of music and nobly played; but it seems, besides, it was a piece peculiar to the Appin Stewarts and a favorite with Alan. Long before the piece was at an end the signs of anger died from him, and he had no thought but for the music.

"Robin Oig," he said, when it was done, "I am not fit to blow in the same kingdom with ye. Though I could maybe show ye another of it with the cold steel, I warn ye beforehand—it'll no be fair! It would go against my heart to haggle a man that can blow the pipes as you can!"

Thereupon that quarrel was made up. All night the pipes were changing hands and the brose was going; and the three men were none the better for what they had been taking, before Robin as much as thought upon the road.

IT WAS ALREADY far through August, and beautiful, warm weather, when I was pronounced able for my journey. Our money was run to so low an ebb that if we came not soon to Mr. Rankeillor's, or if the lawyer should fail to help me, we must surely starve. In Alan's view, besides, the hunt must have now greatly slackened, and the line of the Forth and even Stirling Bridge, the main pass over that river, would be watched with little interest.

The first night, accordingly, we pushed to the house of a Maclaren in Strathire, a friend of Duncan's, where we slept the twenty-first of the month. The twenty-second we lay in a heather bush on the hillside in Uam Var, within view of a herd of deer, the happiest ten hours of sleep in a fine, breathing sunshine that I have ever tasted. That night we struck Allan Water, and coming down to the edge of the hills saw the moon shining on the town of Stirling and the Links of Forth.

"Now," said Alan, "ye're in your own land again. If we could but pass yon crooked water, we might cast our bonnets in the air."

Near where Allan Water falls into the Forth, we found a little sandy islet, overgrown with burdock and butterbur that would just cover us if we lay flat. Here it was we made our camp, within plain view of Stirling Castle, whence we could hear the drums of the garrison. Shearers worked all day in a field on one side of the river, and we could hear even the words of the men talking. It behoved to lie close and keep silent.

As soon as the shearers quit their work and dusk began to fall, we waded ashore and struck for the Bridge of Stirling, keeping to the fields.

The bridge, close under the castle hill, is old, high, and narrow, with pinnacles along the parapet. The moon was not yet up when we came there. A few lights shone along the front of the fortress, and lower down a fewer lighted windows in the town. It was all mighty still, and there seemed to be no guard upon the passage.

"It looks unco quiet," said Alan, "but for all that we'll lie down here cannily behind a dike, and make sure."

So we lay for about a quarter of an hour, hearing nothing but the washing of the water on the piers. At last an old, hobbling woman with a stick came by and set forth up the steep spring of the bridge. She was so little, and the night so dark, that we soon lost sight of her; only heard the sound of her steps and stick draw slowly farther away.

"She's bound to be across now," I whispered.

And just then— "Who goes?" cried a voice, and we heard the butt of a sentry musket rattle on the stones.

"This'll never, never do for us, David," said Alan, and, without another word, he began to crawl away through the fields. A little after, being out of eyeshot, he got to his feet again and struck along a road that led eastward. I could not conceive what he was doing, and besides, I was so sharply cut by the disappointment. A moment back and I had seen myself knocking at Mr. Rankeillor's door to claim my inheritance, like a hero in a ballad; and here was I back again, a wandering, hunted blackguard on the wrong side of Forth.

"Well?" said I. "Why go east?"

"If we cannae pass the river, we'll have to see what we can do for the firth," said he.

"I'm not up to you in talking, Alan," I said; "but I can see if it's hard to pass a river, it must be worse to pass a sea. A river can be swum."

"By them that have the skill of it," returned he; "for my own part I swim like a stone. But on the firth, there's such a thing as a boat."

"Ay, and such a thing as money," says I. "But for us that have neither, they might just as well not have been invented."

"David," says he, "ye're a man of small invention and less faith. If I cannae beg, borrow, nor steal a boat, I'll make one. So deave me with no more of your nonsense, but walk, and let Alan think for ye."

All night, then, we walked, avoiding the towns, and about ten in the morning, hungry and tired, came to the little clachan of

Limekilns. This hamlet by the waterside looks across the firth to the town of Queensferry. Smoke went up from the villages and farms. The fields were being reaped. Boats were coming and going on the firth. And somewhere on the south shore was Mr. Rankeillor's house.

"O, Alan," said I, "to think of it! Over there, there's all that heart could want waiting me. The birds and the boats go over—all that please can go over but just me! O, man, it's a heartbreak!"

In Limekilns we entered a small alehouse and bought some bread and cheese from a good-looking servant lass. This we carried in a bundle, meaning to eat it in a wood on the seashore some third of a mile in front. As we went, Alan fell into a muse. At last he stopped. "Did ye take heed of the lass we bought this of?" says he, tapping the bread and cheese.

"To be sure," said I, "and a bonny lass she was."

"Ye thought that, David?" cried he. "That's good news."

"In the name of all that's wonderful, why so?" says I.

"Well," said Alan, with one of his droll looks, "I was rather in hopes it would maybe get us that boat."

"If it were the other way about, it would be liker it," said I.

"That's all that you ken," said Alan. "I don't want the lass to fall in love with ye, I want her to be sorry for ye, David; to which end there is no need that she should take you for a beauty. Let me see," (looking me over) "I wish ye were a wee thing paler. Apart from that ye'll do for my purpose—ye have a fine hangdog, rag-and-tatter, clappermaclaw look to ye. Come, right about, and back to the alehouse for that boat of ours."

I followed him, laughing.

"David Balfour," said he, "ye're a very funny gentleman, and this is a very funny employ for ye. For all that, I am going to do a bit of playacting and if ye have any affection for my neck (to say nothing of your own) ye will perhaps be kind enough to take this matter responsibly, and conduct yourself according."

"Well, well," said I, "have it as you will."

As we got near Limekilns, he made me take his arm and hang upon it like one almost helpless with weariness. By the time he pushed open the alehouse door, he seemed to be half carrying me. The maid appeared surprised at our speedy return; but Alan spared no words in explanation. He helped me to a chair, called for a brandy which he fed me in little sips, and then, breaking up the bread and cheese, helped me to eat it like a nursery-lass. It was small wonder if the maid were taken with the picture we presented, of a poor, sick overwrought lad and his most tender, concerned comrade.

She drew near, and stood leaning on the next table. "What's wrong with him?" said she at last.

Alan turned upon her with a kind of fury. "Wrong?" cried he. "He's walked more hundreds of miles than he has hairs upon his chin, and slept oftener in wet heather than dry sheets. Wrong, quo' she! Wrong, indeed!" and with his back to her he kept grumbling to himself as he fed me. All this while I was sitting tongue-tied between shame and merriment. But I could hold it no longer, and bade Alan let me be, saying I was better already. My voice stuck in my throat but this very embarrassment helped on the plot, for the lass no doubt set it down to sickness and fatigue.

"He's young for the like of this," she was saying. "He would be better riding."

"And where could I get a horse to him?" cried Alan, turning on her with the same fury. "Would ye have me steal?"

I thought this roughness would have sent her off in dudgeon, but my companion knew very well what he was doing.

"Has he nae friends?" said she, in a tearful voice.

"That has he so," cried Alan, "if we could but win to them!— rich friends, beds to lie in, food to eat, doctors to see to him—and here he must tramp in the heather like a beggarman."

"And why that?" says the lass.

"My dear," said Alan, "I cannae very safely say, but I'll whistle ye a bit tune instead." With that he leaned over the table, and in a mere breath of a whistle gave her a few bars of the Jacobite air, "Charlie Is My Darling."

"Wheesht, and him so young! "cries she, and looked over her shoulder to the door.

"He's old enough to ——" and Alan struck his forefinger on the back of his neck, meaning that I was old enough to lose my head.

"It would be a black shame," she cried, flushing high.

"It's what will be, though," said Alan, "unless we manage the better."

At this the lass turned and ran out of that part of the house, leaving us alone together: Alan in high good humor at the furthering of his schemes, and I in bitter dudgeon at being called a Jacobite, and treated like a child.

"Alan," I cried, "I can stand no more of this."

"Ye'll have to sit it then, Davie," said he. "For if ye upset the pot now, ye may scrape your own life out of the fire, but Alan Breck is a dead man."

This was so true that I could only groan, and even my groan served Alan's purpose, for it was overheard by the lass as she came in again and set before us a dish of puddings and a bottle of ale.

"Poor lamb!" says she, and touched me on the shoulder with a little friendly touch, as much as to bid me cheer up. Then she told us to fall to. There would be no more to pay, for the inn was her father's, and he was away for the day. While we ate, she took up a place by the next table, looking on and frowning to herself, drawing the string of her apron through her hand. "I'm thinking ye have rather a long tongue," she said at last to Alan.

"Ay," said Alan, "but ye see I ken the folk I speak to."

"I would never betray ye," said she, "if ye mean that."

"No," said he, "ye're not that kind. But I'll tell ye what ye would do, ye would help."

"Na, I couldnae," said she, shaking her head.

"No," said he, "but if ye could?" She answered him nothing. "Look, my lass," said Alan. "If we could have a boat to cross the firth under cloud of night, and some secret, decent man to bring that boat back again and keep his counsel, there would be two souls saved—mine to all likelihood—his to a dead surety. If we lack that boat, we have but three shillings left in this wide world, and I kenna what other place there is for us except the gibbet. Shall we go wanting, lassie? Are ye to lie in your warm bed and think upon this poor sick lad, biting his finger ends on a blae muir for cauld and hunger, and with the death grapple at his throat, he must be trailing in the rain on the lang roads; and when he gants his last, there will be nae friends near him, only me and God."

At this appeal, I could see the lass was tempted, yet feared she might be helping malefactors. So I determined to allay her scruples with a portion of the truth. "Did ever you hear," said I, "of Mr. Rankeillor of the Ferry?"

"Rankeillor the lawyer?" said she. "I daursay that!"

"Well," said I, "it's to his door that I am bound. You may judge by that if I am an ill-doer, and I will tell you more. Though I am, by a dreadful error, in peril of my life, King George has no truer friend in Scotland than myself."

Her face cleared up mightily at this, although Alan's darkened.

"That's more than I would ask," said she. "Mr. Rankeillor is a kennt man." And she bade us finish our meat, get clear of Limekilns as soon as might be, and lie close in the wood of elders and hawthorns on the beach. "Trust me," says she, "I'll find some means to put you over."

We shook hands upon this bargain, made short work of the puddings, and set forth to the wood. There we lay all day making the best of the brave warm weather and the good hopes we now had of a deliverance.

At last the night fell, quiet and clear. Lights came out in houses and then, one after another, began to be put out, but it was past eleven, and we were long since tortured with anxieties, before we heard the grinding of oars. We looked out and saw the lass herself rowing to us in a boat. She had trusted no one with our affairs, but as soon as her father was asleep, had left the house, stolen a neighbor's boat, and come to our assistance single-handed.

I was abashed how to find expression for my thanks, but she begged us to hold our peace, saying (very properly) that the heart of our matter was haste and silence. So she set us on the Lothian shore not far from Carriden, and was again rowing back for Limekilns, before there was one word said either of her service or our gratitude.

Even after she was gone, we had nothing to say, as indeed nothing was enough for such a kindness. But later, as we were lying in a den on the seashore, Alan said at last, "It is a very fine lass, David, a very fine lass." For my part, I could still say nothing. My heart smote me both with remorse because we had traded upon her ignorance, and with fear lest we should have involved her in our dangers.

CHAPTER XVI

I come into my kingdom

THE NEXT DAY, it was agreed that Alan should fend for himself till sunset. Then he should hide by the roadside near Newhalls, and stir for naught until he heard me whistling. For this he taught me a little fragment of a Highland air, which has run in my head from that day to this. Every time it comes to me, it takes me off to that last day of my uncertainty, with Alan sitting in the den, whistling and beating the measure with a finger, and the gray of dawn coming on his face.

I was in the long street of Queensferry before the sun was up. As the fires began to be kindled, and the windows to open, and the people to appear out of the houses, my despondency grew ever blacker. I saw that I had no proof of my rights or my identity. And as people looked askance at me in my rags and dirt, nudging or speaking one to another with smiles, I took a fresh apprehension: that it might be no easy matter to come to speech of the lawyer, far less to convince him of my story.

I could not muster up the courage to address any of the reputable burghers, so I went up and down the street, like a dog that had lost its master. By nine in the forenoon, I was worn with these wanderings, and had stopped in front of a very good house with a dog sitting yawning on the step like one that was at home. Well, I was even envying this dumb brute, when the door fell open and there issued forth a shrewd, ruddy, kindly man in a well-powdered wig and spectacles, who, it seems, was so struck with my poor appearance that he came straight up and asked me what I did.

I told him I was come to Queensferry on business, and taking heart, asked him to direct me to the house of Mr. Rankeillor.

"Why," says he, "this is his house, and for a rather singular chance, I am that very man."

"Then, sir," said I, "I have to beg the favor of an interview. My name is David Balfour."

"David Balfour?" he repeated, in rather a high tone, like one surprised. "And where have you come from, Mr. David Balfour?" he asked dryly.

"From many strange places, sir," said I; "but I think it would be as well to tell you where and how in a more private manner."

He mused awhile, looking now at me and now upon the street. "Yes," says he, "that will be the best, no doubt." And he led me back into his house and brought me into a little dusty chamber full of books and documents. Here he sate down, and bade me be seated; though I thought he looked a little ruefully from his clean chair to my muddy rags. "And now," says he, "if you have any business, pray come swiftly to the point. *Nec gemino bellum Trojanum orditur ab ovo*—do you understand that?" says he, with a keen look.

"I will even do as Horace says, sir," I answered, smiling, "and carry you *in medias res*." He nodded as if he was well pleased, and indeed his scrap of Latin had been set to test me.

For all that, and though I was somewhat encouraged, the blood came in my face when I said: "I have reason to believe myself to have some rights on the estate of Shaws."

He got a book out of a drawer and set it before him open. "Well?" said he. But I had shot my bolt and sat speechless. "Come, Mr. Balfour," said he, "you must continue. Where were you born?"

"In Essendean, sir," said I, "the twelfth of March, 1733. My father was Alexander Balfour, schoolmaster of that place, and my mother Grace Pitarrow."

"Have you papers proving your identity?" asked Mr. Rankeillor.

"No, sir," said I, "but they are in the hands of Mr. Campbell, the minister, and could be readily produced. Mr. Campbell, too, would give me his word. For that matter, I do not think my uncle would deny me."

"Meaning Mr. Ebenezer Balfour?" says he.

"The same," said I.

"Did you ever meet a man of the name of Hoseason?" asked Mr. Rankeillor.

"I did so, sir, for my sins," said I. "It was by his means and the procurement of my uncle, that I was kidnapped within sight of this town, carried to sea, suffered shipwreck off the Isle of Mull and a hundred other hardships, and stand before you today in this poor accouterment."

"Ah!" says he smiling. "So far, I may tell you, this agrees pretty exactly with other informations that I hold. But Hoseason's brig was lost on June the twenty-seventh," says he, looking in his book, "and we are now at August the twenty-fifth. Here is a considerable hiatus, Mr. Balfour, of near upon two months."

"Indeed, sir," said I, "these months are very easily filled up. Yet before I tell my story, I would be glad to know that I was talking to a friend. I have already suffered by my trustfulness, and was shipped off to be a slave by the very man that (if I rightly understand) is your employer."

All this while I had been gaining ground with Mr. Rankeillor, and confidence in proportion. At this sally, which I made with something of a smile, he fairly laughed aloud. "No, no," said he, "it is not so bad as that. *Fui, non sum.* I *was* indeed your uncle's man of business; but while you were gallivanting in the west, a good deal of water has run under the bridges. On the very day of your sea disaster, Mr. Campbell stalked into my office, demanding you from all the winds. I had never heard of your existence, but I had known your father, and from matters in my competence I was disposed to fear the worst. Mr. Ebenezer declared, what seemed improbable, that he had given you considerable sums; and that you had started for the continent of Europe, intending to fulfill your education, which was probable and praiseworthy. Interrogated how you had come to send no word to Mr. Campbell, he deponed that you had expressed a great desire to break with your past life.

"I am not exactly sure that anyone believed him," continued Mr. Rankeillor with a smile; "and in particular he so much disrelished

some expressions of mine that he showed me to the door. We were then at a full stand, for whatever suspicions we might entertain, we had no shadow of probation. Then comes Captain Hoseason with the story of your drowning. Whereupon all fell through, with no consequences but concern to Mr. Campbell, injury to my pocket, and another blot upon your uncle's character which could ill afford it. And now, Mr. Balfour," said he, "you can judge for yourself to what extent I may be trusted."

Indeed he was more pedantic than I can represent him, placing many scraps of Latin in his speech. But his fine geniality of manner went far to conquer my distrust and, moreover, I could see he treated me as if my identity was beyond a doubt.

"Sir," said I, "if I tell you my story, I must commit a friend's life to your discretion. Pass me your word that it shall be sacred."

He passed me his word very seriously. "But," said he, "these are alarming prolocutions. If there are in your story any little jostles to the law, I would beg you to bear in mind that I am a lawyer, and pass lightly."

Thereupon I told him my story from the first, he listening with his spectacles thrust up and his eyes closed, so that I sometimes feared he was asleep. But no such matter! He heard every word and years after would remind me of strange Gaelic names heard for that time only. Yet when I called Alan Breck in full we had an odd scene. The name of Alan had of course rung through Scotland, with the news of the Appin murder. It had no sooner escaped me than the lawyer opened his eyes.

"I would name no unnecessary names, Mr. Balfour," said he.

"Well, it might have been better not," said I, "but since I have let it slip, I may as well continue."

"Not at all," said Mr. Rankeillor. "I am somewhat dull of hearing, and I am far from sure I caught the name exactly. We will call your friend, if you please, Mr. Thomson. And I would take some such way with any Highlanders that you may have to mention— dead or alive."

By this, I saw he must have heard the name all too clearly, and had already guessed I might be coming to the murder. If he chose to play this part of ignorance, it was no matter of mine. So I smiled, said it was no very Highland-sounding name, and consented.

"Well, well," said the lawyer, when I had quite done, "this is a great odyssey of yours. You have rolled much. You have shown, besides, a singular aptitude for getting into false positions and, upon the whole, for behaving well in them. It would please me if this Mr. Thomson (with all his merits) were soused in the North Sea, for he is a sore embarrassment, Mr. David. But you are doubtless quite right to adhere to him; indubitably he adhered to you. Well, well, these days are fortunately by; and I think, speaking humanly, that you are near the end of your troubles."

As he thus moralized, he looked upon me with so much humor and benignity that I could scarce contain my satisfaction. I had been so long with lawless people, making my bed under the bare sky, that to sit once more in a clean house, and to talk amicably with a gentleman in broadcloth seemed mighty elevations. Even as I thought so, the lawyer rose, called over the stair to lay another plate, for Mr. Balfour would stay to dinner, and led me into a bedroom. Here he set before me water, soap, and some clothes that belonged to his son, and then left me to my toilet.

I made what change I could in my appearance; and blithe was I to look in the glass and find the beggarman a thing of the past, and David Balfour come to life again. When I had done, Mr. Rankeillor caught me on the stair and had me again into the cabinet.

"Sit ye down, Mr. David," said he. "Now that you are looking more like yourself, let me see if I can find you any news. You will be wondering, no doubt, about your father and your uncle? To be sure, the explanation is one that I blush to offer you. For the matter hinges on a love affair."

"Truly," said I, "I cannot join that notion with my uncle."

"But your uncle, Mr. David, was not always old," replied the lawyer, "and what may perhaps surprise you more, not always ugly. He had a fine, gallant air, and a spirit of his own that seemed to promise great things in the future. However, eventually he and your father fell in love, and that with the same lady. Mr. Ebenezer, who was the admired and spoiled one, made, no doubt, mighty

certain of the victory, and when he found he had deceived himself, screamed like a peacock. The whole country heard of it. Now he lay sick at home; now he rode from public house to public house, and shouted his sorrows into the ear of Tom, Dick, and Harry. Your father, Mr. David, was a kind gentleman, but he was dolefully weak and took all this folly with a long countenance.

"The end of it was, that from concession to concession on your father's part, and from one height to another of squalling selfishness upon your uncle's, they came at last to a sort of bargain. The one took the lady, the other the estate. Now, Mr. David, I often think that in this life the happiest consequences flow when a gentleman consults his lawyer, and takes all the law allows him. Anyhow, your father's piece of quixotry, as it was unjust in itself, has brought forth a monstrous family of injustices. Your father and mother lived and died poor folk. You were poorly reared. In the meanwhile, what a time it has been for the tenants of Shaws! And I might add (if it was a matter I cared much about) what a time for Mr. Ebenezer! For those who knew the story gave him the cold shoulder. Those who knew it not, seeing one brother disappear, and the other succeed in the estate, raised a cry of murder. Upon all sides he found himself avoided. Money was all he got by his bargain. Well, he came to think the more of money. He was selfish when he was young, he is selfish now that he is old."

"Well, sir," said I, "and in all this, what is my position?"

"The estate is yours beyond doubt," replied the lawyer. "It matters nothing what your father signed. But your uncle is a man to fight the indefensible. It would be likely your identity that he would call in question. A family lawsuit is always expensive and scandalous. Besides, if any of your doings with your friend Mr. Thomson were to come out, we might find that we had burned our fingers. The kidnapping, to be sure, would be a court card upon your side, but it may be difficult to prove. My advice is to make a very easy bargain with your uncle, perhaps even leaving him at Shaws, and contenting yourself meanwhile with a fair provision."

I told him I was very willing to be easy. Meantime (thinking to myself) I began to see the outlines of that scheme on which we afterwards acted. "The great affair," I asked, "is to bring home to him the kidnapping?"

"Surely," said Mr. Rankeillor, "and if possible, out of court."

"Well, sir," said I, "here is my way of it." And I opened my plot to him.

"But this would involve my meeting the man Thomson," says he, rubbing his brow. "No, Mr. David, I am afraid your scheme is inadmissible. I know nothing against your friend but if I did—mark this, Mr. David!—it would be my duty to lay hands on him. Now I put it to you: is it wise to meet? He may not have told you all."

"You must be the judge, sir," said I.

But it was clear my plan had taken his fancy, for he kept musing to himself till we were called to midday dinner and the company of Mrs. Rankeillor. That lady had scarce left us again to ourselves and a bottle of wine, ere he was back harping on my proposal. He kept asking questions at long intervals, while he thoughtfully rolled his wine upon his tongue. When I had answered all of them, seemingly to his contentment, he got a sheet of paper and a pencil, and set to work writing, weighing every word. At last he touched a bell and had his clerk into the chamber. "Torrance," said he, "I must have this written out fair against tonight. When it is done, you will be so kind as to come along with this gentleman and me, for you will probably be wanted as a witness."

"What, sir," cried I, as soon as the clerk was gone, "are you to venture it?"

"Why, so it would appear," says he, filling his glass. "But let us speak no more of business. The very sight of Torrance brings in my head a little droll matter of some years ago, when I had made a tryst with the poor oaf at the cross of Edinburgh. When it came four o'clock, Torrance had been taking a glass and did not know his master, and I, who had forgot my spectacles, was so blind that I give you my word I did not know my own clerk." And thereupon he laughed heartily.

I said it was an odd chance, and smiled out of politeness. But all the afternoon, he kept telling this story with fresh details and laughter, so that I began to feel quite ashamed for his folly.

Towards the time I had appointed with Alan, Mr. Rankeillor and I set out from the house, and Torrance followed behind with the deed in his pocket and a covered basket in his hand. All through the town, the lawyer was bowing right and left, and continually being buttonholed by gentlemen on matters of business, and I could see he was one greatly looked up to in the county.

At last we were clear of the houses, and began to go along the side of the haven and towards the Hawes Inn and the ferry pier. This was the scene of my misfortune, and I could not look upon the place without a chill of recollected fear, and sorrow for the many who had been there with me that day and were now no more.

I was so thinking when, upon a sudden, he clapped his hand to his pockets, and began to laugh. "Why," he cries, "if this be not a farcical adventure! After all that I said, I have forgot my glasses!"

At that, I understood the purpose of his anecdote. If he had left his spectacles at home, it had been done on purpose, so that he might have the benefit of Alan's help without the awkwardness of recognizing him. For all that, he had recognized a good few persons as we came through the town, and I had little doubt that he saw reasonably well.

As soon as we were past the Hawes Inn, I went forward in the manner of a scout, whistling my Gaelic air, and at length I had the pleasure to see Alan rise from behind a bush. He was somewhat dashed in spirits, having passed a long day alone skulking in the country. But at the mere sight of my clothes he began to brighten up, and as soon as I had told him in what a forward state our matters were, and the part I looked to him to play in what remained, he sprang into a new man.

"That is a very good notion of yours," says he, "and I dare to say that you could lay your hands upon no better man to put it through than Alan Breck. But it sticks in my head your lawyer will be somewhat wearying to see me."

Accordingly I waved to Mr. Rankeillor, who came up alone and was presented to my friend, "Mr. Thomson, I am pleased to meet you," said he. "But I have forgotten my glasses, and Mr. David, here, will tell you that I am little better than blind; so you must not be surprised if I pass you by tomorrow. And now as you and I are the chief actors in this enterprise, I propose that you should lend me your arm, for (what with the dusk and the want of my glasses) I am not very clear as to the path. As for you, Mr. David, you will find Torrance a pleasant kind of body to speak with. Only let me remind you it's quite needless he should hear more of your adventures or those of—ahem—Mr. Thomson."

Accordingly these two went on ahead in very close talk, and Torrance and I brought up the rear.

Ten o'clock had been gone some time when we came in view of the house of Shaws. It was dark and mild, with a pleasant, rustling wind that covered the sound of our approach. As we drew near we saw no glimmer of light in the building. It seemed my uncle was already in bed. The lawyer, Torrance, and I crouched down quietly beside the corner of the house. As soon as we were in our places, Alan strode to the door and began to knock.

For some time his knocking only roused the echoes of the house. At last, however, I could hear a window gently thrust up and the quavering voice of my uncle. "This is nae time of night for decent folk. What brings ye here? And whae are ye? I have a blunderbush."

"Is that yourself, Mr. Balfour?" returned Alan, stepping back and looking up into the darkness. "I have no inclination to rowt out my name to the countryside. But what brings me here is another story."

"And what is't?" asked my uncle.

"David," says Alan.

"What was that?" cried my uncle, in a mighty changed voice.

"Shall I give ye the rest of the name, then?" said Alan.

There was a pause. Then, "I'm thinking I'll better let ye in," says my uncle, doubtfully.

"I daresay that," said Alan, "but I am thinking that it is upon this doorstep or nowhere that we must confer, for I am as stiff-necked as yoursel', and a gentleman of better family."

Ebenezer was a little while digesting this change of note, and then says he, "Weel, weel, what must be must," and shut the window. But it took him a long time to get downstairs and undo the fastenings, repenting (I daresay) and taken with fresh claps of fear at every second step and every bolt. At last, however, the door hinges creaked, and my uncle slipped gingerly out and (seeing that Alan had stepped back a pace or two) sate down on the doorstep with the blunderbuss ready in his hands. "If ye take a step nearer," says he, "ye're as good as deid. And now that we understand each other, ye can name your business."

"You will have perceived that I am an Hieland gentleman," says Alan. "My name has nae business in my story, but my country is no very far from the Isle of Mull, of which you will have heard. It seems there was a ship lost in those parts, and the next day a gentleman of my family came upon a half-drowned lad along the sands. Well, he brought him to and clapped him in an auld castle, where from that day to this he has been a great expense to my family. My relatives are not particular about the law; and finding that the lad was your nephew, Mr. Balfour, they asked me to give ye a call. I may tell ye at the off-go, unless we can agree upon terms, ye are little likely to set eyes upon him. For my relatives are no very well off."

My uncle cleared his throat. "I'm no very caring," says he. "I take nae interest in the lad and I'll pay nae ransom."

"Hoot, sir," says Alan. "Blood's thicker than water! Ye cannae desert your brother's son for the shame of it. If ye did, and it came to be kennt, ye wouldnae be very popular in your countryside."

"I'm no very popular the way it is," returned Ebenezer; "and I dinnae see how it would come to be kennt onyway."

"It'll be David that tells it," said Alan.

"How's that?" says my uncle sharply.

"Ou, just this way," says Alan. "If there was nae likelihood of siller to be got by keeping him, I'm thinking that my friends would let him gang where he pleased, and be damned to him. But by all that I could hear, there were two ways of it; either ye liked David and would pay to get him back; or else ye had good reasons for not wanting him, and would pay us to keep him. It seems it's not the first; well then, it's the second, and blithe am I to ken it. It should be a pretty penny in my family's pockets."

"I dinnae follow ye there," said my uncle.

"No?" said Alan. "See here: you dinnae want the lad back. Well, what do you want with him, and how much will ye pay?"

My uncle shifted uneasily on his seat.

"Come, sir," cried Alan. "I bear a king's name. I am nae traveler to kick my shanks at your door. Either give me an answer in civility; or by the top of Glencoe, I will ram three feet of iron through your vitals."

"Eh, man," cried my uncle, scrambling to his feet, "give me a meenit! I'm just a plain man and I'm trying to be as ceevil as possible. As for that wild talk, it's disrepitable. Vitals, says you! And where would I be with my blunderbush?"

"Powder and your jottering hands are but as the snail to the swallow against the bright steel in the hands of Alan," said the other. "Troth, sir, I ask for nothing but plain dealing. Do ye want the lad killed or kept?"

"O, sirs!" cried Ebenezer. "That's no kind of language. We'll have nae blood shed, if you please."

"Well," says Alan, "as ye please; that'll be the dearer."

"The dearer?" cries Ebenezer. "Would ye fyle your hands wi' crime?"

"Hoot!" said Alan. "They're baith crime! And killing's easier. Keeping the lad'll be a troublesome job."

"I'll have him keep it, though," returned my uncle. "I'm a man o' principles and if I have to pay for it, I'll pay for it. Besides, ye forget the lad's my brother's son."

"Well, well," said Alan, "you're unco scrupulous. But now the price. It's not very easy for me to name it. I would first have to ken, for instance, what ye gave Hoseason for kidnapping David."

"It's a black lee!" cried my uncle. "He was never kidnapped. He leed in his throat that tauld ye that. Did Hoseason tell ye?"

"Why, ye donnered auld runt, how else would I ken?" cried Alan. "Hoseason and me are partners. We gang shares, so ye can see for yoursel' what good ye can do leeing. The point in hand is just this: what did ye pay him?"

"Weel," said my uncle, "I dinnae care what he said; God's truth is that I gave him twenty pound. But I'll be honest with ye: forby that, he was to have the selling of the lad in Caroliny, whilk would be as muckle mair, but no from my pocket, ye see."

"Thank you, Mr. Thomson. That will do excellently," said the lawyer, stepping forward, and then, mighty civilly, "Good evening, Mr. Balfour."

And, "Good evening, Uncle Ebenezer," said I.

And, "It's a braw nicht, Mr. Balfour," added Torrance.

Never a word said my uncle, but just stared upon us like a man turned to stone. Alan filched away his blunderbuss, and the lawyer led him by the arm into the kitchen, whither we all followed, and set him down in a chair beside the hearth. The fire was out and only a rushlight was burning.

"Come, come, Mr. Ebenezer," said the lawyer, "you must not be downhearted, for I promise we shall make easy terms. Meanwhile give us the cellar key, and Torrance shall draw us a bottle of your father's wine in honor of the event."

Then, turning to me and taking me by the hand, "Mr. David," says he, "I wish you all joy in your good fortune, which I believe to be deserved."

Soon we had the fire lighted, and a bottle of wine uncorked. A good supper came out of the basket, to which Torrance, Alan, and I set ourselves down, while the lawyer and my uncle passed into the next chamber to consult. At the end of an hour they had come to an understanding, and my uncle and I set our hands to the agreement in a formal manner. By the terms of this, my uncle bound himself to satisfy Rankeillor for his services, and to pay me two-thirds of the yearly income of Shaws.

So the beggar in the ballad had come home, and when I lay down that night on the kitchen chests, I was a man of means and had a name in the country. Alan, Torrance, and Rankeillor slept and snored on their hard beds; but for me who had lain out under heaven and upon dirt and stones so many days and nights, this good change in my case unmanned me more than any of the former evil ones, and I lay till dawn, looking at the fire on the roof and planning the future.

CHAPTER XVII

Good-by!

SO FAR AS I WAS CONCERNED, I had come to port. But I had still Alan, to whom I was much beholden, on my hands, and I felt besides a heavy charge in the matter of the Appin murder and James of the Glens. On both these heads I unbosomed to Rankeillor next morning, walking to and fro before the house of Shaws.

About my duty to my friend, the lawyer had no doubt. I must help him out of the country at whatever risk. But in the case of James, he was of a different mind. "Mr. Thomson," says he, "is one thing, Mr. Thomson's kinsman quite another. I know little of the facts, but I gather that the Duke of Argyle has some concern and even feels some animosity in the matter. If you interfere to balk his vengeance, you should remember there is one way to shut your testimony out; that is to put you in the dock. And to be tried for your life before a Highland jury, on a Highland quarrel and with a Highland judge, would be a brief transition to the gallows."

Now I had made all these reasonings before and found no very good reply to them, so I put on all the simplicity I could. "In that case, sir," said I, "I would just have to be hanged—would I not?"

"My dear boy," cries he, "do what you think is right. It is a poor thought that at my time of life I should be advising you to choose the safe and shameful, and I take it back with an apology. Go, do your duty, and be hanged, if you must, like a gentleman."

I saw I had pleased him heartily, and when we turned into the house he wrote me two letters, making comments on them as he wrote. "This," says he, "is to my bankers, the British Linen Company, placing credit to your name. I trust you will be a good husband of your money, but in the affair of a friend like Mr. Thomson, I would be even prodigal. Then for his kinsman, there is no better way than that you should seek the Lord Advocate, tell him your tale, and offer testimony. Whether he will take it or not will turn on the Duke of Argyle. That you may reach the Lord Advocate well

120

recommended, I give you here a letter to the learned Mr. Balfour of Pilrig. It will look better that you should be presented by one of your own name, and the laird of Pilrig stands well with the Lord Advocate. May the Lord guide you, Mr. David!"

Thereupon he took his farewell, and set out with Torrance for the Ferry, while Alan and I turned for Edinburgh. As we went, we kept looking back at the house of my fathers. It stood there, great and smokeless, like a place not lived in. Only in one of the top windows the peak of a nightcap was bobbing up and down, like the head of a rabbit from a burrow. I had little welcome when I came, and less kindness while I stayed, but at least I was watched as I went away.

Alan and I had little heart either to walk or speak, for both knew that we were near the time of parting. The remembrance of all bygone days sate upon us sorely. We talked of what should be done, and it was resolved that Alan should bide now here, now there, but come once a day to a particular place where I might communicate with him by messenger. Meanwhile, I was to seek out an Appin Stewart lawyer, a man to be trusted, to arrange for Alan's safe embarkation. No sooner was this business done, than the words seemed to leave us. Though I would seek to jest with Alan under the name of Mr. Thomson, and he with me on my new estate, you could feel very well that we were nearer tears than laughter.

When we came over a hill, near to the place called Rest-and-be-Thankful, and looked over to Edinburgh, we stopped. We both knew without a word said that we had come to where our ways parted. Here he repeated to me once again what had been agreed upon between us, and I gave what money I had (a guinea or two of Rankeillor's) so that he should not starve in the meanwhile. Then we stood a space, and looked over in silence at the city and the Castle on the hill.

"Well, good-by," said Alan, and held out his hand.

"Good-by," said I, and gave the hand a little grasp, and went off down the hill.

Neither one of us looked the other in the face, nor did I take one back glance. But as I went on my way to the city, I felt so lost and lonesome that I could have found it in my heart to sit down and weep like any baby.

It was near noon when I passed into the streets of the capital. The huge height of the buildings, the narrow arched entries that continually vomited passengers, the wares of the merchants in their windows, the hubbub and endless stir, struck me into a kind of stupor of surprise, so that I let the crowd carry me to and fro. Yet all the time what I was thinking of was Alan at Rest-and-be-Thankful; and all the time there was a cold gnawing in my inside like a remorse for something wrong.

The hand of Providence brought me in my drifting to the very doors of the British Linen Company's bank.

Editor's Note

"Just there," says Stevenson in an editorial aside, "with his hand upon his fortune, the present editor inclines for the time to say farewell to David. How Alan escaped, and what was done about the murder, with a variety of other delectable particulars, may be some day set forth. That is a thing, however, that hinges on the public fancy."

"The public fancy" did not for long leave the author in doubt. Soon he was at work on a sequel, to be called *David Balfour* and to become almost as famous as its predecessor. In it are recounted the further adventures of our hero and of the intrepid Alan Breck Stewart, of which it will here be enough to say—as Stevenson said—"that whatever befell them, it was not dishonour, and whatever failed them, they were not found wanting to themselves."

Other Titles by
Robert Louis Stevenson

The Black Arrow. New York: Scribner's, 1987.

A Child's Garden of Verses. New York: Macmillan, 1981.

The Strange Case of Dr. Jekyll and Mr. Hyde. New York: Bantam, 1981.

The Master of Ballantrae. Emma Letly, editor. New York: Oxford University Press, 1983.

The Moon. New York: Harper & Row, 1984.

The New Arabian Nights. Boston: Shambhala Publications, 1986.

Travels With a Donkey; An Inland Voyage; The Silverado Squatters. Totowa, NJ: Biblio Distributors, 1978.

Weir of Hermiston & Other Stories. Paul Binding, editor. New York: Penguin, 1980.

The Wrong Box. London: Amereon, 1979.